Thomas Marc Parrott

An Examination of the Non-Dramatic Poems in Robert

Brownings first and second periods

Thomas Marc Parrott

An Examination of the Non-Dramatic Poems in Robert Brownings first and second periods

ISBN/EAN: 9783337342104

Printed in Europe, USA, Canada, Australia, Japan

Cover: Foto ©Andreas Hilbeck / pixelio.de

More available books at **www.hansebooks.com**

AN EXAMINATION

OF

THE NON-DRAMATIC POEMS

IN

ROBERT BROWNINGS FIRST AND SECOND PERIODS, TO WHICH IS ADDED A BIBLIOGRAPHY

BEING PART OF A THESIS

PRESENTED

TO THE PHILOSOPHICAL FACULTY

OF THE UNIVERSITY OF LEIPZIG

FOR THE

DEGREE OF DOCTOR OF PHILOSOPHY

. BY

THOMAS M. PARROTT.

————————→←————————

LEIPZIG-R.
PRINTED BY OSWALD SCHMIDT
1893.

K
᷉

TO MY PARENTS

THESE FIRST FRUITS.

PREFACE.

The following study does not pretend to be an exhaustive treatment of Browning. It is simply an attempt to discover those of his poems in which his dramatic method, which colors the great body of his work, is lacking, and from these to extract by careful examination his beliefs on the great questions of life. The theory of life which may be extracted and arranged from these does not completely correspond to Browning's, for as I have shown in this study, he prefers as a rule to teach indirectly and by means of his dramatic method. But it has the advantage over all presentations which have yet been made of being grounded solely upon poems in which the poet gives direct utterance to his beliefs, and not upon a method of miscellaneous quotation from poems dramatic or otherwise. And I believe that while certain dramatic poems add detail and color to his beliefs, they contain no essential point that will not also be found in the poems I have examined. As it is over the religious and ethical beliefs of Browning that the bitterest controversy has occurred, I have examined these with great care and, I hope, impartially; but my work throughout has been that of the student of literature rather than of theology or philosophy, and my aim has been rather to ascertain the theory of life held by a poet who was also a profound thinker, than to criticise the formulated system of a theologian or philosopher, neither of which Browning was.

The references throughout are to the standard edition of Browning's works in 16 volumes, published 1888—1889 by Smith, Elder & Co., and to *Asolando*, 1889 by the same house. I quote by volume and page, giving where possible the stanza (st.) and paragraph (§). In quoting from the *Ring and the Book* I give book and line. I have used throughout the following abbreviations; *Para.* = *Paracelsus*, *Sord.* = *Sordello*, *B. and P.* = *Bells and Pomegranates*, *M. and W.* = *Men and Women*, *Dram. Pers.* = *Dramatis Personae*, *R. and B.* = *Ring and the Book*, *P. H. S.* = *Prince Hohenstiel Schwangau*, *R. C. N. C.* = *Red Cotton Night Cap Country*, *L. S.* = *La Sosiaz*, *Jocos.* = *Jocoseria*, *Parley.* = *Parleyings with certain People*, *Aso.* = *Asolando*. In the notes I have constantly used B. = Browning. In quoting from works on Browning it is my practise to give by the first reference, the full name of work, date of publication &c., by subsequent reference merely the name of the author and the page of his work. The works cited under the names of Mrs. Orr and Dr. Berdoe, in regard to which confusion might arise, are Mrs. Orr's Life of Browning, and Dr. Berdoe's Browning Cyclopedia, unless otherwise stated. I refer to the papers of the Browning Society (London) under the abbreviation Brown. Soc. Pap., quoting by pact and page.

CONTENTS.

INTRODUCTION.

Browning's position in Victorian Literature and his relation to his time.

No poet of the Victorian Era better deserves or repays careful and conscientious study than Robert Browning. It is not too much to say that he demands such study. Without literary parentage or progeny his position in the literature of the last half-century is so unique that where such study is omitted he is sure to be misunderstood; and the result is unmeasured and uncritical denunciation or equally unmeasured and uncritical praise.[1]

In the dreary waste of Browning literature it is but seldom that we come upon a critic who is at once impartial and understanding. Most of the earlier criticisms are unworthy of the name, being mere bursts of eulogy or execration, and even when the critic evidently desires to be impartial, there is too often a lack of sympathy,

---

[1] Even as able a critic as Stedman has fallen into these faults and his characterisation of B. in the 1st edition of Victorian Poets (Boston 1875) is a masterpiece of misconception, whereas in the 2nd and revised edition (Boston 1887) he has allowed himself to be carried away by the rising tide of popular admiration for the poet, and praises almost as indiscriminately as he had blamed before. It is incomprehensible how a critic who has denounced *Dramatis Personae* as "uncouth and puerile" can bestow unqualified praise on the vastly inferior work of Jocoseria.

a consideration of the subject from a false standpoint, which vitiates his wellmeant work.[2]

The inability of criticism to deal with the problems presented by a poet marks always a new appearance in the field of art and thought. That which is old is understood, is received or rejected according to its deserts. That which is new may be praised or blamed. It is only the most understanding minds that will comprehend it before it has become old. It is interesting to notice in this relation the difference between the reception of Tennyson and Browning at the hands of the critics throughout a practically contemporaneous course. Tennyson represents confessedly the union of the principles which dominated Wordsworth and Keats, combining the simplicity of feeling of the older with the rich color and metrical mastery of the younger poet. And so Tennyson's work was from the first, in spite of a hostile review or two received and *appreciated at its worth*. But Browning represents no such well known principles. Mr. Fotheringham in his appreciative study of Browning[3] has sought to ·bring him into connection with Shelley, Wordsworth, and Keats, but except in the case of the first named it would he hard to find traces of their influence save in the most general way, and although Shelley's influence is much more discernible, there remains, after all his influence be subtracted, more than enough distinctly Browning's own to make him a new figure in English Literature.

And as Browning was without literary parentage

---

[2] As examples of such criticism may serve Bagehot's essay on "Wordsworth, Tennyson, and Browning or Pure, Ornate, and Grotesque Art in Poetry" in "Literary Studies"—Bagehot. (London 1879), v. 2, pp. 338—390, or R. H. Hutton's essay in his "Literary Studies" (London 1888) pp. 188—224. The 1st of these is written from the standpoint of the old fashioned classicist whose highest conception of act is realized in the cold purity of Wordsworth's Sonnets; the 2nd is by Bagehot's literary disciple, whose sympathies have been extended far enough to embrace Tennyson, but who is quite out of touch with the realism of to-day.

[3] Studies in the Poetry of R. B. J. Fotheringham. London 2nd ed. 1888.

so he seems to have passed away without leaving a
school behind him. Traces of his mode of thought are
indeed visible everywhere in the literature of to-day;
essays, sermons, criticisms of life, show often an adapta-
tion evidently only half-conscious, of the liberal, ideal
spirit of Browning; and traces of his manner are to
be seen distinctly in such poems as[4] Rossetti's *A Last
Confession* and *Jenny*, and Tennyson's *Rizpah* and *Colum-
bus*. And in Robert Buchanan's *"The Outcast"* we have
an exaggerated imitation of Browning's most careless
manner without the pungency of thought and consciousness of strength which gives worth to Browning's matter
in its worst form.

But in the case of his influence upon his con-
temporaries and followers, as in the case of the influence
of his predecessors on him, when all is said, Browning
still remains a unique figure in the literature of this
century. And as such be demands the carefuller study,
for it is only through himself that he can be understood.

This solitary position of Browning's has led to a
commonplace of criticism, that he was out of sympathy
with his age. Like most commonplaces this is a half-
truth, and like most half-truths it produces a wholly
false impression. Browning was, it is true, essentially
the poet of the inner, rather than the outer life of
man. In a period of production which extends from
1833 to 1889, embracing such events as the Reform
Bill, the Repeal of the Corn-laws, the Chartist movement,
the revolutions which convulsed Europe in 1848—1849,
the rise and fall of the Second Empire, the liberation
of Italy, the Crimean War, the tremendous struggle
which freed the slaves, and settled the question as to
nationality or federation in the United States, the
resurrection of the German Empire,—in all these years,
teeming with such wonderful births, and in the quieter
years that followed them, we have no pamphlets on

---

[4] R's Poem's. Tauchnitz Edition pp. 58 and 109. The Works
of T. Macmillan and Co. New York 1884. pp. 604 and 628.

chartism, no poems on the charge at Balaclava, nor
odes on the openings of International Exhibitions, no
L'Année Terrible, no *"Ilias Americana in Nuce"*. Even
in the political question which most strongly appealed
to him the liberation of Italy, we have but to compare
his occasional references, with the passionate appeals,
paeans of premature triumph, and wails of disappointed
hope, which his wife poured forth to see where his
heart lay. While Europe was racked with the last
great struggle between Absolutism and Liberty, he
was writing his rhapsodies of Christmas Eve and Easter
Day on the nature and worth of religious belief; while
the reconstruction of Germany was in process, he was
arresting with the problem of evil, and evolving from
a record of unutterable villainy the characters of Pompilia and the "soldier saint" Giuseppe Caponsacchi;
while the Eastern Question was troubling the mind of
Europe, he was meditating on the bearings of the
doctrine of personal immortality on the conduct of life.[5]
But to assume that Browning was a hermit, with-drawn
from the world and all its affairs, is demonstrably false.
His poems are filled with allusions to contemporary
persons, and political and social events, allusions which
may escape the careless eye, but show the careful
reader of his poems, that these are the work of a man,
who is well aware of the world about him, and uses
it as the material of his thought. From a much greater
number of allusions that might be cited, I have chosen
the following to substantiate my assertion that Browning's mind was impregnated with the color of the world
he lived in, and that be turned from the world, not as
indifferent to it, but because he felt the things that
are within, of higher importance to man, than those
that are without.

---

[5] La Sasiaz 1878.

Allusions to contemporary persons and events.

A) Royal personages, statesmen &c.

I. Persons.

Francis I of Austria	v.	3	p.	52
Charles Albert of Sardinia	„	5	„	48
Victor Emanuel	„	14	„	116
Ferdinand II of the Two Sicilies	„	4	„	267
Louis Napoleon[6]	„	11	„	—
Empress Eugenie	„	13	„	149
Duchesse de Berri	„	13	„	145
Comte de Chambord	„	13	„	145
Metternich	„	3	„	49
Buol	„	7	„	246
Gortschakoff	„	7	„	246
Cavour	„	7	„	246
Bismarck	„	13	„	137
Guizot	„	6	„	169
Montalembert	„	6	„	169
Rouher	„	13	„	137
Roon	„	13	„	137
Ollivier	„	13	„	137
Gambetta	„	14	„	163
Marshall McMahon	„	14	„	163
Gladstone	„	13	„	201
Disraeli	„	13	„	203
Antonelli	„	4	„	267
Thiers	„	11	„	173
Radetzky	„	6	„	89
Rothschild	„	13	„	194

B) Authors and Philosophers.

Carlyle[7]	v. 13	p. 201

---

[6] The entire poem P. H. S. is an examination in B's dramatic method of the principles on which the conduct of Napoleon III was based. cf. B's remarks on Napoleon III in his letter to Miss Blagden (Mrs Orr p. 291).

[7] "My venerated friend, Thomas Carlyle . . . his dear and noble name" Prefatory note to the Agamemnon of Aeschylus (v. 13, p. 267) cf. Mrs. Orr p. 82, 134, 172—173, 365 as to B's relations to C.

Tennyson[8]	v.	13	p.	201
Cardinal Newman	"	4	"	267
Dickens	"	4	"	276
Miss Barrett	"	11	"	121
Matthew Arnold	"	12	"	264
Ruskin	"	13	"	193
Antony Trollope	"	13	"	234
Walter Savage Londor[9]	"	6	"	207
Miss Thackerey	"	13	"	5
Heine	"	7	"	87
Balzac	"	4	"	242
Dumas père	"	13	"	88
Dumas fils	"	13	"	254
Victor Hugo	"	11	"	173
Béranger[10]	"	13	"	63
J. Milsand[11]	"	13	"	122
Veuillot	"	13	"	149
St. Beuve	"	16	"	199
Quicherat	"	16	"	199
Silvio Pellico	"	3	"	52
Proudhon	"	11	"	156
Comte	"	11	"	142
Fourier	"	11	"	142
Renan[12]	"	13	"	149
Darwin	"	16	"	161
Schelling	"	4	"	254
Strauss	"	4	"	261
Emerson	"	7	"	234
Lowell	"	7	"	241

---

[8] Mrs. Orr p. 203. T. reads *Maud* to the B's and Rossetti.

[9] B. and P. no. 8, including *Lucia* and *A Soul's Tragedy*, is dedicated to W. S. L. For B's relations to him see Mrs. Orr p. 83, 105, 224 ssq., 228 ssq. 392 no. 10.

[10] cf. Mrs. Orr, p. 377.

[11] An intimate friend of B's, who was first drawn to him his discriminating review of Para., B. and P., C. E. and E. D. in the Revue des Deux Mondes. *"Parleyings"* is dedicated to his memory.

[12] R. is made the 2nd speaker in the Epilogue to *Dram. Pers.*

Hawthorne	v. 7	p. 241
Longfellow.[13]	„ 7	„ 241

C) Painters, Sculptors, Musicians &c.

Corot	v. 13	p. 184
Ingres	„ 7	„ 77
Frederick Leigthon	„ 7	„ 170
Doré	„ 11	„ 250
Gêrome	„ 11	„ 257
Meissonier	„ 11	„ 168
Woolner	„ 7	„ 167
Gibson	„ 7	„ 171
Pugin	„ 4	„ 238
Liszt	„ 13	„ 170
Paganini	„ 13	„ 16
Dvorak	„ 16	„ 225
Brahms	„ 16	„ 225
Gounod	Aso.	„ 103
Raff	v. 13	„ 234
Czerny	„ 13	„ 234
Wagner	„ 13	„ 311
Schumann	„ 11	„ 302
Bellini	„ 5	„ 64
Auber	„ 5	„ 64
Verdi	„ 4	„ 253
Rossini	„ 4	„ 253
Grisi	„ 7	„ 171
Jenny Lind	„ 7	„ 234
Salvini	„ 11	„ 271

[13] This list might be largely extended I chose to quote from Mrs. Orr to show the relations of the poet to the literary world of his day, but I have preferred to confine myself here, as throughout this study, to his works.

II. EVENTS.

A. Political.

B. Social Movements, Events &c.

---

[14] cf. the whole tom of Carlyle's *Post and Present* 1843.

[15] Note B's sure conviction of the expulsion of the Austrians expressed as early as 1855; v. 6, p. 89.

[16] The transcendental Philosophy of Kant and his followers, introduced into England by Coleridge, Carlyle and Emerson, seems to have had a strong, though only mediate effect on B. The success at Fichte and Schelling in the poem quoted here are not B's. own opinions, but dramatically most appropriate to Bishop Bloughram.

[17] The Mesmerism of 1855 represents the beginnings of the investigation into Hypnotism. See Berdoe's note on this poem, p. 272.

— 17 —

The growth and influence of Journalism in the last half century does not escape Browning's notice and he refers to

Handicrafts of the day are noticed

---

[18] *Bishop Bloughram's Apology* has been frequently misunderstood. It neither states B.'s attitude with regard to matters of faith, nor his opinion of the leaders of a certain form of faith. A review of M. and W. (in which this poem is included) in the Romanist journal, *The Rambler* (Jan. 1856), charges B. with having in this poem caricatured Cardinal Wiseman. These are undoubtedly points of resemblance between Bishop Bloughram and the Cardinal, but B. hardly meant to assert that the opinions he puts into the mouth of the Bishop were those of the Cardinal. They are not even the true opinions of the imaginary Bishop, as a reference to the 2nd section of p. 277, v. 4 shows. As far as the poem is anything but a study in dialectics, with passages of high poetic power (p. 245 for example), it expresses B.'s preference for the man who puts his theory of life, be it what it may, into practice over the man who is too cowardly or indolent to realize his ideal. Gigadibs, the literary man, who represents a very common phase of indolent, indifferent unbelief, is beaten at every point by Bloughram, worldly and low-minded as the latter is. He feels this himself, rouses himself from his dilettante efforts at literary work, and emigrates to Australia to put into practice Carlyle's Gospel of Work. That Cardinal Wiseman may have sat for the portrait of the Bishop as Wordsworth did for that of the "Lost Leader", is quite possible. But that Bloughram is the "very effigies" of Cardinal Wiseman B. would have been the first to deny. I have cited this poem not to show B.'s attitude toward the Catholic revival in England, but simply his cognizance of it.

2

| Leipzig printing[19] | v. 4 | p. 242 |
| Kensington Exhibitions | „ 13 | „ 15 |

Amusements of a young "man about town"
v. 7 pp. 178—9
v. 13 p. 194

The following references, collected by Dr. Berdoe (pp. 469—470) from the separate editions of Browning's poems, I have carefully revised and reduced to the standard of the edition of 1888—9. They show Browning's acquaintance with the Natural Science of the day.

1. Anatomy.

| Circulation of the blood | v. 5 | p. 248 |
| Dissection | „ 7 | „ 65 |

2. Astronomy.

| Moon and tides | v. 1 | p. 256—7 |
| Orb and satellites | v. 11 | p. 176 |

3. Botany.

Rose and the parasite aphis	v. 11	p. 290
Ferns—their variety	„ 5	„ 295
Borage—its nitrous qualities	„ 4	„ 197
Lily-pollen and insectivorous plants	„ 11	„ 231
Fertilization of flowers by insects	v. 6	p. 194—5

4. Chemistry.

Extraction of dye-stuffs	v. 6	p. 195
White dye from black ingredients	„ 11	„ 150
Smelting of ore	„ 5	„ 117
Testing of a peace	„ 5	„ 252
Chemical elements shown by color of flame	v. 14	p. 211—2

---

[19] Little Greek books with the funny text. They get up well at Leipzig.

Effect of acid on alkali	v. 11	p. 290
A chemical experiment	„ 15	„ 51
Crystals in salt marshes	„ 1	„ 264
Acid and alloy	K. and B. b. I, ll. 23—5	

5. Electricity.

In a cat	v. 7	p. 206
Means of producing it	v. 7	p. 228—9
Conductors and non-conductors	v. 13	p. 125
Snap of spark from knuckle	„ 11	„ 303

6. *Evolution* is alluded to in the following passages
v. 1, p. 168; v. 7, p. 228; v. 11, p. 164; v. 11, p. 337;
v. 14, p. 189; v. 16, p. 182 &c.

7. Optics.

Reference to the prism	v. 6	p. 125
Newton's theory of colors	„ 11	„ 267
Decomposition of light	„ 11	„ 241

The whole poem *Numpholeptos* v. 14, p. 263—9 is
an allegory whose figures are drawn from the science
of Optics.

8. *Materia Medica and Therapeutics.* Various allusions in v. 15, p. 129; v. 11, p. 169; v. 12, p. 126.
Tincture of Laudanum v. 2, p. 81.

9. Miscellaneous.

Physiology, process of nerve formation	v. 5	p. 292
Microscopy, lowest forms of life	„ 7	„ 228
Atoms, their properties	„ 16	„ 84
Entomology	v. 1, p. 76 and v. 13 p. 168—9	
Acoustic laws and chemical change	v. 10	p. 119
Vivisection[20]	v. 15, p. 57 and Aso. p. 56.	

[20] Browning was strongly opposed to Vivisection, an opposition which seems rather to have proceeded from the natural kind-
ness of his heart than from any understanding of the question.

2*

Enough has been quoted to substantiate my assertion that Browning was in touch with the world of his day, and to show that, if he did not devote himself to its political or social movements, nor attempt to solve the problems which these called up, it was not from lack of sympathy with his time. It was rather because he felt that the greatest movements and the only true answer to the problems lay within. He believed as little in machinery for perfecting the race as did Carlyle. It is not the outer but the inner life that concerns Browning, not men's actions but the motives which underlie, cause, and, when apprehended, explain these. What was the ideal, how was it realized in life? These are the questions that press upon him for solution when any character appears within the field of his poetic vision. And the greater bulk of his work is devoted to the answer of these questions in the case of the most widely different characters. And in each case that which appeals to him is the same—the inner life, action in character, "incidents in the developement of a soul".[21] In each case his aim is the same—to find in this inner life the interpretation of the outer life which is assumed as known.[22] This aim he pursues with an ardor, a persistence and an objectivity which may well be compared to the spirit of the scientific investigator testing facts to establish his hypothesis. Browning was in fact a scientific student of the soul. To this study he devoted the whole of his productive

---

The 2 poems cited are as remarkable for their misconceptions of its claims as for their lack of poetic merit.

[21] Preface to the 1863 edition of Gordello. v. 1, p. 49.

[22] Among the most striking examples of this aim is B.'s treatment of the character of Strafford. Macaulay had stigmatised him as a renegade, the Lucifer of the Revolution. B. sought to free him from this charge by revealing 2 leading motives, conviction of the necessity of absolute monarchy (Prose Life of Strafford), and devotion to the person of the monarch (Strafford a Tragedy), which remove the charge of inconsistency and explain if they do not justify his course. And such an authority on the period as Prof. Gardiner (in his introduction to Miss Hickey's edition of Strafford) declares that B. has depicted the real Strafford.

life, beginning with experiments and investigations, and reaching definite results. What these results were I have endeavored in the following pages to show.

CHAPTER FIRST.

Difficulties in the way of ascertaing Browning's theory of life—His dramatic method.

Two difficulties lie in the way of an attempt to present concretely and systematically Browning's theory of life.

First the too-often-forgotten fact that he was first of all a poet and not a metaphysician or moral philosopher. His poetry at its best was written for its own sake, not for the lesson it should convey. That he often, especially in his later years, departed from this principle of pure act is undeniable; but to attempt to read moral lessons into all his work, more especially into such creations of the pure imagination as *Childe Roland*,[23] for example, is to violate the first principles

---

[23] Berdoe pp. 103 ssq. gives a number of these. Mr. Kirkman holds that the poem describes allegorically the sensations of a sick man very near to death. Mr. Nettleship (Robert Browning, Essay and Thoughts, revised edition London 1890) sees in it a picture of the inevitable disappointment attendant on the realization of a cherished ideal. Mrs. Bagg (Berdoe p. 104) draws a confused moral lesson from it. "Some have seen in the poem an allegory of Love, others of the search after Truth. Others again understand the Dark Tower to represent Unfaith, and the obscure land that of Doubt" Berdoe p. 104. Berdoe's own view, that the poem is a picture of the Age of Materialistic Science and a protest against Vivisection, is the most untenable of all. All these views are brought forward by their respective partisans in spite of B.'s repeated declaration to Dr. Furnival that the poem was simply a dramatic creation called forth by a line of Shakespeare's (King Lear III, 4). This statement is given in Berdoe p. 103.

of literary criticism. The widely different interpretations which have been given of the supposed hidden meaning of this poem prove of themselves the absence of any such meaning. When Browning has wished to convey a moral lesson, as in *The Statue and the Bust*, there is no question as to his meaning.[24] The real difficulty for the student lies not in any hidden meaning but rather in the fragmentary, disconnected, and at times, in consistent character of Browning's theory of life. This is an inevitable consequence of the poetic form in which it appears; the more unity connection, and consistency there is in the presentation of his views, the more the poetic form must be disregarded for the metaphysical or moral matter which it presents. It was only toward the end of his life that Browning completely neglected form for the sake of a more explicit statement of his philosophy, and Prof. Jones,[25] the most careful and impartial critic of the philosophy of Browning, asserts (p. 343) that the worth of this philosophy is in direct ratio to the value of the poetic form. With the single exceptions of *Ferishtah* and *Parleyings* Browning has written nothing that may be considered as a systematic

---

Mrs. Orr says very properly "We may recognize in the poem a poetic vision of life . . . The thing we may not do is to imagine that an intended lesson is conveyed by it (Handbook to the Works of R. B. (London 1885), article on Childe Roland.

[24] Such attempts to discover a leading moral idea in a particular volume and by main force fit all the poems of that volume into the Procrustean bed, as the Rev. J. Sharpe's (Brow. Soc. Pap. v. 1, p. 191) in the case of Dramatic Idylls II, and Berdoe's (p. 560) in the case of Jocoseria, would be merely laughable were it not for the ridicule which they bring at once upon all literary criticism and upon the poet they are maltreating. If such a simple lyric as "Wanting is—What? (v. 15, p. 167) may be made to convey the doctrine of the Incarnation because the epithet "comer" which occurs in it corresponds to ὁ ἐρχόμενος, one of the titles applied in the New Testament to Christ, there is no liberty which interpretators of B. may not take. And from this strained interpretation Berdoe gets the scheme to which he fits all the poems of *Jocoseria*.

[25] B. as a Philosophical and Religious Teacher. 2nd edition. Glasgow 1892.

and more or less complete Confession of Faith. His
theory of life is to be constructed from hints, allusions,
and single utterances scattered throughout his work,
and the inconsistencies that appear are to be explained
either as due to his developement beyond a standpoint
once adopted or as due to the influences of temporary
moods. The consistency we demand of a philosopher
we need hardly expect to find in a poet.

The second difficulty which confronts us, Browning's
dramatic method, naturally calls up the question as to
his position as a dramatic poet as far as his dramas
proper are concerned, this question may be regarded
as settled by such criticisms as those of M. Milsand,[26]
M. Sarrazin,[27] and Mr. Sharpe.[28] The Drama proper,
written for the stage, is not Browning's field. That he
was not a master of the technique of the stage is shown
by such errors as the practical absence of the figure
of Strafford from the 4th act of the tragedy which
bears his name, by the long, involved parenthetical
speech of Guendolen[29] to Austin at a moment which
calls for the simplest and most direct appeal, even more
clearly by the beautiful, but ridiculously icetimed serenade
of Mertown.[30] It may be urged in Browning's defence,
as has been done by the actor and manager, Lawrence
Barrett[31] that such faults were due to the inexperience
of a young playwright and would have been overcome
had the conditions of the English stage encouraged
Browning to continue work for it. But there is a graver
fault in his plays than the mere lack of technical skill,
a fault which no amount of experience would have

---

[26] Revue des Deux Mondes 1851, p. 661 ssq. La Poésie anglaise
depuis Byron—II—Robert Browning.
[27] Renaissance de la Poésie anglaise. Paris 1889.
[28] Great Writer Series—Robert Browning. London 1890.
[29] A Blot &c. v. 4, pp. 45—47.
[30] A Blot &c. v. 4, p. 21.
[31] See the Introduction to Rolfe and Hersey's ed. of "A Blot &c.
New York 1887. I see that Stedman in his last work "The
Nature and Elements of Poetry" (Boston 1892) p. 110, takes the
same view.

removed. This is the air of remoteness which makes itself felt in all of them (with the one exception of the *Blot on the Scutcheon*). The characters do not act immediately upon us, we see them through a medium which adds to their distinctness and charpness of outline but detracts from their lifelike reality. We admire or condemn the persons and the motives of their actions but they are too far away from us to evoke real sympathy. And this quality of remoteness makes itself nowhere so strongly felt as in Browning's last and most carefully finished drama, Luria. It is therefore more than doubtful if he would ever have overcome this fault. That the poet himself felt this is shown, I believe, by his entire abandonment of the drama proper after 1846. *In a Balcony*, 1855, is, as it were, the 5th act of a lost drama. As it stands, it is no more a drama than the *Sebald and Ottiana* scene in *Pippa*. The Prologue and Epilogue to the *Parleyings* are mere caprices in rhymed stanzas, and cannot be seriously criticised as dramas.

But Browning's dramatic method extends far beyond the range of his dramas proper, and being, as premised, one of the difficulties in the way of ascertaining his personal beliefs, it now calls for careful consideration. Where does this method show itself? In that great body of his work to which M. Sarrazin has given the name of la psychologie dramatique. "Il substitue" says M. Sarrazin, "les causes aux effets, et au théâtre extérieur, c'est à dire à l'aboutissement de l'âme, le théâtre intérieur, c'est à dire, l'âme elle-même".[32] What is meant by the assertion that Browning took for his theatre the soul itself? Not only that he discarded the conventionalities and paraphernalia of the stage as no longer suiting the dramatic genius of this age; but also that he adopted a new method. The drama presents us objective character, not the poet's own, in a process of self

---

[32] Prof. Corson (Introduction to B., Boston 1886) sees in this work of Browning's a realization of the drama anticipated by Mrs. Browning in Aurora Leigh pp. 163—164. Tauchnitz edition.

revelation. This is effected by the interaction of the various characters of the drama. Their deeds rather than their words show us what they are, Browning's "drama of the soul" also presents us with objective character in a process of self revelation. And this is still effected by the interaction of the characters but with him the action is that of mind on mind. The speeches of Browning's dramatis personae represent not so much spoken words as mental processes. A passage from R. C. N. C. (v. 12, p. 138), in which Browning breaks off narration for a moment, throws light upon this method

"He thought —
  (Suppose I should prefer "He said"?
Along with every act and speech is act
There go, a multitude impalpable
To ordinary human faculty,
The thoughts which give the act significance.
Who is a poet needs must apprehend
Alike both speech and thoughts which prompt to speak.
Pact these and thought with draws to poetry
Speech is reported in the newspaper.)"

He said, then, probably no word at all. But thought as follows,—in a minute's space then follows a passage of 12 pages most inappropriate if regarded as the last words of Miranda, most appropriate if regarded as an attempt to give by words, and such as he would have used had he spoken all that was passing in his mind, a picture of his mental condition. This is "la psychologie dramatique". Bearing this in mind we understand passages that would otherwise seem most unreal if nor ridiculous. In *R. and B.* book VI, for example, Caponsacchi is called tor the second time before his judges to repeat the story of his feight with Pompilia. In ll. 437—439 he tells us of a talk with a friend, on the evening after he had first seen her, who spoke of her husband's jealousy and unkindness and advised him to shun her company. Nothing can be more absurd than to imagine Caponsacchi repeating to the bench of judges his friend's speech with its snatches of intoned Latin. But if we understand the words as we are meant to do, as embodying not only what the speaker said, but also what he thought while speaking, the absurdity disappears and the passage becomes intensely realistic as showing how every incident, even the least, connected with Pompilia was so impressed upon the young priest's mind that the mere mention of it calls up all its attendant circumstances.

Thus thought has in Browning's dramatic method the same function as physical action in the drama proper, it reveals to us the character which lies behind the thought as well as the act. But inasmuch as thought is more closely related to, and more strongly colored by, the character than is outer action, it is, on that account, a better mirror of the character. The difficulty lies in obtaining a result which will be accepted as a picture of the mind as acted upon by other minds. To obtain this result Browning has invented the Dramatic Monologue, a form which is by no means to be confounded with the soliloquy which is in its nature undramatic and often tends to run into the lyric.[33] The best definition that we have of this form is given by Prof. Johnson (Brown. Soc. Pap. pt. III p. 279).

The dramatic monologue differs from a soliloquy in this, while there is but one speaker, the presence of a second silent person is supposed, to whom the arguments of the speaker are addressed. It is obvious that the dramatic monologue gains over the soliloquy in that it allows the artist greater room in which to work out his conception of character; the thoughts of a man in self communion are apt to run in a certain circle, and to assume a monotony. The introduction of the second person, acting powerfully upon the speaker throughout, draws the latter forth into a more complete and varied expression of his mind, and the silent person in the background, who may all the time be master of the

---

[33] For example the famous opening soliloquy of *Faust*, especially the passage beginning "O, sähst du, voller Mondenschein &c." which the lamented Prof. Zarncke aptly called "eine lyrische Partie".

situation, supplies a powerful stimulus to the imagination of the reader." To this it may be added that the charácter of the second person may also be revealed to us mediately by its operation upon the speaker as is the case with Lucrezia in *Andrea*, Gigadibs in *Bishop Bloughram*, and Elvire in *Fifine*. The interaction of character which is thus introduced, whether expressly brought out or merely indicated, heightens the interest and gives to this form a dramatic value far superior to the soliloquy. Prof. Alexander[34] gives a study of this form which is worthy of longer examination than space permits me to give. He points out its superiority to the psychological novel and soliloquy as a revealer of the soul, but calls attention to 2 drawbacks, which he considers inevitable, the high degree of analytical power that it assumes on the part of the speaker, and the lack of independent beauty in the separate parts of such poems. But the first objection falls to the ground when we remember that such poems represent not only spoken words but mental conditions, and the analytical ability rests therefore with the poet[35] not the speaker. And the compression which makes each part dependent on the whole is to many the special and stimulating charm of Browning.

Prof. Alexander illustrates the working of this

---

[34] Introduction to B. Boston 1889. pp. 9—20.

[35] It is quite impossible, for example that Shakespeare's Caliban should have spoken the words which B. puts into his mouth in the poem, *Caliban upon Sete bos* (v. 7, p. 149), but it is quite as impossible that he should have spoken in verse. In every creation of act, the maker impacts something of his personality to his creatures. B. has in this case entered into the mind of Caliban, and arranged the vague half-formed conceptions which he found there. The poem represents the result, being the self-revelation of a character upon whom the poet had bestowed the gift of ordered thought. All that we have the right to demand is that the mental state or process revealed to us shall be consistent with the character to whom it belongs. The question in regard to this poem, for example, is not whether Caliban would have the power to utter such thoughts as are there found, but whether these are consistent with the character of Caliban as we know him from Shakespeare.

dromatic method by an examination of *My Last Duchess*. An even better example would be *Andrea del Sarto*, a poem which I regard as Browning's most finished specimen of the dramatic monologue. He finds in the story of Andrea's life as given by Vasari, a true tragedy of the soul, a conflict between duty and passion, the victory of the latter, and the ensuing moral ruin of the whole character. Instead of casting the story into the old dramatic or the narrative form, he has placed it in the mouth of Andrea himself, and so obtained an immediate revelation of the soul with allusions that give us the preceeding events and with premonitions of the approaching end of the drama. The first four lines give us the keynote of the situation, the soft yielding character of Andrea, the over bearing disposition of his wife and the passion to which he had sacrificed all, but the hopelessness of which he is now beginning to realize. Little touches as the poem progresses emphasize this passion and its lack of spirituality. He suspects that she has never truly loved him, knows that the pride she once had in him is gone, and feels that she has never given him the sympathy that would have stirred him to nobler effort in his art (p. 226). He more than half suspects her infidelities (p. 229), and yet in spite of all he is fascinated by her charms with all an artist's passion[36] for the beautiful. Touch by touch the story of his life comes out, his early promise which evoked the praise of Michel Angelo (p. 228), his year at Fontainebleau when under the patronage of Francis I he had the opportunity of fulfilling this promise (p. 227), his departure at the insistence of his wife, his betrayal of the confidence reposed in him by his patron, and his shame and dread of meeting the "Paris lords" (p. 226). We see the despair that comes from opportunities wasted, aims unaccomplished, a life

---

[36] Note the allusions to Lucrezia's beauty, her hand, ears, face, brow, eyes, mouth hair and low voice (v. 4, pp. 222, 225, 226, and 228).

unfulfilled. Against this despair he takes refuge in a numbing fatalism

> Love, we all in God's hand.

How strange now looks the life, &c. (p. 223). And the last line of the poem indicates the approaching end when he will be deprived of even the semblance of that love for which he gave up all, deprived too without a struggle, having fallen too low to resist.

I have spoken at some length of this poem because it shows us in a concrete form the results obtained by Browning's dramatic method at its best. We have perfect objectivity (the fatalism of Andrea is the exact opposite of the poet's personal belief), and the self revelation of Andrea's character, of what it has been, is now, and will sink to, is complete. And the character of Lucrezia is as completely developed, although she never says a word, unless the exclamation "What he?" (p. 228 2nd line from the bottom) be taken as Andrea's wondering repetition of a question put by her. This revelation is effected however not by the old method of allowing as to judge character from outward actions but by opening as it were a window through which we may see into the soul itself. It is not only Andrea's words that we hear. His very thoughts lie open to us and these in turn reveal immediately his character, and mediately that if his evil genius, Lucrezia. And this result is obtained and can he obtained in such a degree only by Browning's special method of the monologue.

The term dramatic monologue is not used by Browning himself, but he applies the adjective "dramatic" to a number of poems classed under the heads of dramatic lyrics, dramatic romances, and dramatic idylls. Browning was not very accurate in the nomenclature of his poems nor does he seem to have been very well satisfied with it, as the frequent changes of arrangement show. Of the 14 poems entitled *Dramatic Lyrics* which constitute the 3rd number of *B. and P.* we find but 4 included under the *Lyrics* of the edition of 1863, the others

being assigned to the *Dramatic Romances* and the group
entitled *Men and Women.*[37] To the third number of
B. and P. Browning prefixed the following note which
is reprinted with but a slight change in the last edition
of his works (v. 6, p. 3), "Such poems as the following
come properly enough, I suppose under the head of
"Dramatic Pieces"[38] being though often lyrical in expression, always dramatic in principle and so many
utterances of so many imaginary persons, not mine".
This declaration of the poet, however, it is impossible
for us to accept literally. Of the 47 poems included
in the last edition under the heading, "Dramatic Lyrics",[39]
15 cannot by any stretch of the definition of a lyric
be considered as such. And as to their being *always*
the utterances of imaginary persons, *The Guardian Angel*
(v. 6, p. 187) is addressed to Browning's friend, Mr.
Alfred Dommett, then in New Zealand, contains a distinct
allusion to Mrs. Browning, and is a record to the visit
of the poet-pair to Fano. The speaker can not possibly
be other than the poet himself. *By the Fireside* (v. 6,
p. 126) is undoubtedly[41] autobiographical; and notwith-
standing the poet's declaration it is impossible for students
of his life and thought to believe that such poems as

---

[37] The name of the volume of 1855 was from 1863 on used
to designate a group of 12 (from 1868, 13 poems).

[38] The reference is to the Advertisement to the 1st no of B.
and P.

[39]
       Ghent to Aix
       Garden Francis II
       Soliloquy of the Spanish Cloister
       The Confessional
       Up at a Villa &c.
       Old Pictures at Florence
       Sane
       By the Fireside
       Any Wife to Any Husband
       A Pretty Woman
       Before
       After
       The Guardian Angel
       Popularity.

[40] Mrs. Orr pp. 159—160.

[41] See my examination of this poem [unprinted].

The Lost Leader (v. 6, p. 7), *Home Thoughts from Abroad*
(v. 6, p. 95), *Home Thoughts from the Sea* (v. 6, p. 97),
Old Pictures &c. (v. 6, p. 77) and *De Gustibus* (v. 6,
p. 92) are other than the utterances of the poet himself. Since, then, this confusion of nomenclature exists,
let us try as simply as possible to rectify it. We may
include under the head of Dramatic Lyrics such poems
as are the song-like expression of a single mood, the
mood, however, being not the poet's own but that of
an imaginary or historical character in whom the poet
has sunk his own personality. It is this abandonment[42]
of the personal standpoint that gives these lyrics the
objective quality which Browning has wished to denote
by calling them "dramatic". To this category belong
not only the poems included under the head of *Dramatic Lyrics* in the last edition of Browning, but many of
the poems found in *Dram. Per., Pacch., Jocos.* and *Aso.*

Under the head of *Dramatic Romances* we may include
such poems as are essentially narrative in form, containing
an incident, or incidents, about which the thoughts
and reflections gather. The poem is put in the mouth
of some actor in the events narrated (*Childe Roland*
v. 5, p. 194), or some eye witness of these (*The Glove*
v. 5, p. 36). Here, as in the dramatic monologue, the
poet sinks his own personality, and in so far employs
his dramatic method. The gain in vividness of presentation is apparent.

Of the *Dramatic Idylls* (v. 15) some would naturally
fall under the definition of the Dramatic Romance
(*Martin Relph, Clive*), others are simple narrations by
the poet himself (*Halbert and Hob, Ned Bratts*). It is

---

[42] A comparison of Shelley's famous "*When the lamp is
shattered* with B's *Misconceptions* (v. 6, p. 154) shows the difference
between the personal and the dramatic lyric. Both poems give
lyrical expression to the same theme—the flight of love; but
Shelley's we know to be addressed to Mrs. Williams and to be an
out pouring of his own soul; whereas Browning's, written in 1855
or somewhat earlier, during the happiest period of his married
life, can not possibly be regarded as his own utterance, but is
that of an imaginary character.

evident that in these last the poet has attached another meaning to the term, "dramatic", and applied it to these idylls, not to denote their objective quality, but rather the abundance of action and realistic portrayal of life which distinguishes them from the ordinary idyll.

Under these 3 heads, the Dramatic Monologue, Lyric, and Romance we may include all the poems in which Browning employs, to a greater or less extent his dramatic method.

To return to the difficulty of discovering Browning's personal views from which the necessity of examining his dramatic method has led us, I assert that the revelation of thought or character in such poems is not to be taken as the poet's own.

Browning has repeatedly protested against such a reading of himself into his works.

His first poem Pauline includes as an antidote to its subjective Shelleyan character, a note supposed to be written by the Pauline to whom the confession is addressed. And this note (v. 1, p. 36) contains a bit of objective criticism of the poem of which Shelley would never have been capable. In the preface to the revision of the poem for the collected edition of 1868, Browning once more emphasizes the objective character of the poem; "The thing was my earliest attempt at *poetry always dramatic in principle* and *so many utterances of so many imaginary persons not mine* . . . a sketch that, on review, appears not altogether wide of some hint of the characteristic features of that particular *dramatis persona* it would fain have reproduced" (vol. I, unpaged 2 pages after title-page). That the personal element enters largely into *Pauline* is capable of proof, as I hope to show hereafter. Indeed it could hardly have been otherwise with a poem written by a youth of twenty under the immediate influence of Shelley; but we may not take *Pauline* as it stands and without further proof as an revelation of Browning's character and embodiment of his views at the time of its composition.

The title of the volume of 1864, *Dramatis Personae*, is meant to indicate its objective character as is shown by Browning's use of the same phrase in his preface to the revised *Pauline* of 1868. In the *Pacchiarotto* volume, 1876, the poet protests repeatedly against this identification of himself with his creations. In *"At the Mermaid"* (v. 14, p. 33), he puts these words into the mouth of Shakespeare who as I shall show hereafter is only the mouth piece of Browning's own views.

> Which of you did I enable
> Once to slip inside my breast
> There to catalogue and label
> What I like least, what love best.
> Hope and fear, believe and doubt of
> Seek and shun, respect—deride?
> Who has right to make a rout of.
> Rarities he found inside?
> — — — — — — — —
>   be content I baulk
> Him and you, and bar my portal!
> Here's my work outside: opine
> What's inside me, mean and mortal
> Take your pleasure, leave me mine.

And again in *"House"* v. 14, p. 39.

> Shall I sonnet sing you about myself?
> Do I live in a house you would like to see?
> Is it scant of year, has it store of self?
> "Unlock my heart with a sonnet key"?
>
> Invite the world as my betters have done?
> "Take notice: This building remains on view
> Its suites of reception every one
> Its private apartment, a bedroom too;
>
> For a ticket apply to the publisher."
> No: Thanking the public I must decline.
> A peep through my window if folk prefer;
> But, please you, no foot over threshold of mine!
> — — — — — — — — — — — —

'*With this same key Shakespeare unlocked his heart*',[43] once more! Did Shakespeare? If so the less Shakespeare

---

[43] These words are supposed to be uttered by friends remonstrating with the poet on his indisposition to reveal himself in song. The quotation is from Wordsworth.

he! In the Epilogue to *Pacchiarotto* (o. 14, pp. 141—152)
where Browning defends himself against the attacks of
the critics who stigmatize his verse (spoken of as wine),
as too harsh for the public taste, there is a passage in
which they suggest that this harshness might be removed,
if the poet would consent to flavor his wine with flowers,
i. e. introduce particulars of his private life into his
work.   He answers (p. 150—151)

> And, friends, beyond dispute
> I too have the cowslips dewy and dear.
> Punctual as Springtide forth peep they;
> I leave them to make my meadow gay.
> But I ought to pluck and impound them, eh?
> - - - - - - - - - - - - -
> What if I sacrifice?
> If I out with shears and shear, nor stop
> Shearing till prostrate, lo, the crop?
> And will you prefer it to gingerpop
> When I 've made you wine of the memories
> Which leave us bare as a churchyard tomb
> My meadow late all bloom?
>
> Nay what ingratitude
> Should I hesitate to amuse the wits
> Who have pulled so long at my flask nor grudged.
> - - - - - - - - - - - - -
> Grateful or ingrate—none,
> No cowslip of all my fairy crew
> Shall help to concoct what makes you wink
> And goes to your head till you think you think.
> I like them alive.

In the Digression in Sordello v. 1, pp. 156—172
Browning introduces to as two types of the poetic
genius.   Of the first whom he has already embodied in
the person of Eglamor he says (p. 156—7 Note):

> In just such songs as Eglamor wrote[44]
> With heart and soul and strength for he believed
> Himself achieving all to be achieved
> By singer, in such songs you find alone
> Completeness, judge the song and singer one,
> And either purpose answered, his in it

---

[44] cf. *Essay* p. 6 and 7.

Or its in him; while from true works — — —
— — — — — — — — — — — — — — — —
                  escapes their still
Some proof the singer's proper life was 'neath
The life his song exhibits. — — — — — —
— — — — a passion and a knowledge far
Transcending[45] these, majestic as they are,
— — — — his lay was but an episode
In the bard's life."

From the quotations already made it seems clear that it was to this latter class that Browning considered himself as belonging. And it would seem needless to insist on the impropriety of quoting at random from his works and using such quotations as representing the poets own opinions were it not that this practice is so common as to render necessary the most decided protests on the part of those who desire simply to discover *what* the poet himself believed and are careless as to the exact form of philosophical or religious creed which his would-be interpreters are anxious to thrust upon him.

In the debate for example which followed the reading of Mrs. Glazebrook's 1st paper before the Browning Society[46] one member asserted that the poet must be a Christian or he never could have said of the Apostle John

                  now the man
Lies, as he lay once, breast to breast with God.[47]

If this ardent defender of the faith had examined the poem more closely he would have found that these words are spoken by an early Christian on the eve of martyrdom, "Seeing that I to-morrow fight the beasts"[48] and are in his mouth most appropriate, but prove absolutely nothing as to the poets views on the immor-

---

[45] i. c. his works.
[46] Part 9, see Abstract of proceedings.
[47] v. 7, p. 147.
[48] v. 7, p. 147.

tality of the soul or the divinity of Christ. In the same way the occasionally quoted passage

"I never realized God's birth before[49]
How He grew likest God in being born"

is most natural in the mouth of the deeply religious Pompilia, but in no way testifies to the poet's personal belief.

Even such a careful student of Browning as Prof. Jones quotes whatever suits his purpose with far too little thought whether the passage be of a dramatic or personal character. A few examples may suffice. Two of the 3 passages quoted on p. 172 to illustrate Browning's estimate of the potency of love are the words of Valence,[50] the lover par excellence. To quote Valence without farther discussion as expressing Browning's views is about as accurate as to quote Falstaff's estimate of honor as expressing Shakespeare's. On p. 92 he sees in the oft-quoted passage

The acknowledgement of god in Christ,[51]
Accepted by thy reason solves for thee
All questions in the earth and out of it.

An expression of the poet's own conviction. Now the poem from which these lines are taken is a dramatic monologue[52] and, until it is proved that the speaker (St. John) is a mere mouth-piece of the poet, to quote from it leaves the citer open to the charge of wilfully using dramatic language as the poets own. Again he quotes, p. 241, from L. S. (v. 14, p. 193)

Take the joys and hear the sorrows, neither with extreme concern,
Living here means nescience simply; 'tis next life that helps
to learn.

This passage is at once suspicious on account of its indifferentism which is strikingly at variance with

---

[49] R. and B. book 7 ll. 1690—91.
[50] *Colombe's Birthday* v. 4, pp. 165—166.
[51] *A Death* &c. v. 7, p. 139.
[52] See Nettleship's opinion of the poem p. 375.

Browning's usual attitude, and an examination of the context shows that it is not an affirmatory, but a hypothetical statement.[53] His quotations on p. 247 and pp. 253—4 from *A Beau-Stripe* (v. 16, p. 80 and p. 70) are not the words of the poet, but those of an imaginary scholar who is rebuked for them by Feristah, the latter representing, throughout the series which bears his name, the poet himself. In the same way the quotations from *Bernard de Maudeville* on p. 254 and p. 317 (v. 16, p. 119 and p. 123) do not express the opinions of the poet but those of a confirmed pessimist whom Browning, with the aid of Maudeville, is attempting to confute.

Prof. Alexander is hardly guilty of such miscellaneous quotation, but he builds up almost his whole theory of Browning's relation to Christianity[54] on the dramatic monologues of *Karshish* (v. 4, p. 186 ssq.) and *A Death* &c., to which he adds a passage from R. and B. (book 10, ll. 1361—1414), without however attempting to justify his identification of the speaker, Pope Innocent, with the poet, and a short passage from *C. E.* (v. 5, pp. 250—251), the only passage of those he has quoted which has the authority of a direct personal expression of Browning's. Again on p. 59 Prof. Alexander adds a foot-note to his reprint of *Pisgah-Sights* II (v. 14, p. 51) to explain that the sentiment of the line
Sage our desistence[55]
is dramatic only, not Browning's; because, probably it seems to him a contradiction of Browning's usual principle of striving against evil.

But of a poem can be quoted in support of a given view, as this poem is here quoted by Prof. Alexander, and at the same time one line containing a sentiment which fails to meet the approval of the quoter can be calmly labelled dramatic and struck out of the poem, there is an end of all impartial literary interpretation.

---

[53] See my examination of this poem, p. 237 ssq., below (unprinted).

[54] Alexander pp. 60 ssq.

[55] Namely from trying to remedy the evil in the world.

It is plain, I think, that if we are to consider Browning as a moral teacher, some other ground must be taken as a starling point, than that which has been hitherto adopted. The method of random quotation leads to absurdities when pushed to its logical extreme, for if we may identify the poet with any one of his characters without showing reason therefore, we may identify him with any other, and place in his mouth the incarnate selfishnesses of Guido, the cringing meaness of Mr. Sludge, or the worldly wisdom of Bishop Bloughram. And if we are to make a distinction between dramatic figures which do and those which do not give utterance to the poet's personal beliefs, between dramatic poems which are in their aim didactic, and those which are purely dramatic, mere studies of character, we must first of all look for a criterion which will justify us in making such a distinction. That Browning meant to convey a lesson in many of his dramatic poems I have no doubt, a lesson not directly conveyed, but the more stimulating on that account. At the close of R. and B. (book 12, ll. 836 &c.) he says,

So British Public — — — — — — — — — —
— — — — — — — — — — — —
                    learn one lesson hence
Of many which whatever lives should teach:
This lesson that our human speech is nought
Our human testimony false, our fame
And human estimation words and wind.
Why take the artistic way to prove so much?
Because it is the glory and good of Art
That Art remains the one way possible
Of speaking truth, to mindslike mine, at least.
How look a brother in the face and say
"Thy right is wrong, eyes hast thou yet art blind,
Thine ears are stuffed and stopped despite their length,
And oh the foolishness thou countest faith!

Such direct preaching, he continues, must fail of its aim; not only does is rouse the anger of him to whom it is addressed, but the very truth meant to be imparted becomes infected with the imperfect medium of words in which it is conveyed, "truth looks false".

On the other hand the indirect method may attain
its aim

> Art—wherein man nowise speaks to men[56]
> Only to mankind—Art may tell a truth
> *Obliquely, do the thing shall breed the thought*
> *Nor wrong the thought missing the mediate word.*
> So you may paint your picture twice show truth
> Beyond mere imagery on the wall
> — — — — — — — — — — — — — — — —
> So write a book shall mean beside the facts,
> Suffice the eye and save the soul beside.

It was, I believe, this high estimation of the value
of the artistic presentation of truth, as well as his
own predilection for the dramatic form which led him
to cast the greater part of his work into this shape.
But before it is possible to examine his dramatic poems,
it is necessary that we have firm ground to stand on,
that a criterion be found which may be applied to these.

CHAPTER SECOND.

Non-dramatic poems of Browning—Periods of his work.

I have shown the impropriety of quoting at will
from the dramatic poems of Browning. I have shown
also that he believed truth could be best conveyed by
the indirect method. But while this method has the
advantage of stimulating independent thought, it has
the corresponding disadvantage of leaving the poet's
own thought unrevealed. For without corroborative
testimony it is impossible to claim views advanced in
the dramatic poems as the poet's own. This corroborative
testimony, this firm ground from which we may safely

---

[56] i. e. to separate individuals, as a preacher to his parishioners.

proceed to examine the dramatic works, it is the purpose of this study to discover and investigate.

There are, I believe, in the mass of Browning's work 2 kinds of poems from which we may ascertain his personal views, without laying ourselves open to the charge of confusing the personal with the dramatic element.

I. Poems, or passages, in which the dramatic element is altogether lacking, in which there is no revelation of objective character, no" stress laid on the incidents in the developement of a soul"; but which are purely subjective, giving us directly the opinions of the poet. Such poems are scattered at intervals through his earlier work, are found more frequently after *R. and B.*, and constitute the distinguishing characteristic of his last period. To these poems must be added his *Essay* on *Shelley* which is of the highest value as a direct expression of his deepest convictions.

II. Poems, or passages, which, though dramatic in form, are personal in content; where the "imaginary person" serves as a mere mouth-piece for the poet himself. Care must be taken in dealing with this class, not to fall into the mistake already censured of disregarding the dramatic method. I have, however, included in this class only such poems as may be proved by internal or external evidence to be the utterances of the poet, or such whose dramatic impropriety awakes the suspicion that we are dealing here with subjective rather than objective work. And the final court of appeal for these poems must be their agreement with the ideas embodied in those of the 1st class.

By a careful and impartial examination of all poems belonging to these 2 classes it is possible te obtain results from which a systematic theory of life may be constructed, which will indisputably claim acknowledgement as the poet's own. And by a comparison, with this standard, of his dramatic poems we may discover in them such similar trains of thought, as will show truth

Beside mere imagery.

and reveal to us the meaning that lies "beside the facts."

Such a comparison the limits of this study have not allowed me to make, but I believe that I have established a standard which renders it possible.

In my examination of the following poems I have purposely avoided any rubrics such as God, Nature, Art, &c. under which citations from various poems might be grouped. Such a method awakes the suspicion that the quotations have been chosen to suit the arranger's purpose, and that an examination of the works from which they are drawn, *might* reveal other passages which would tell against those chosen for quotation. Again such an arrangement demands more or less of criticism of the views presented under the various rubrics. I avoid any such suspicion by examing at such length as may be necessary all the poems I have chosen, giving merely at the close of my investigation a brief recapitulation of the facts discovered. A discussion of the ethical and philosophical value of the theory of life contained in these facts I have altogether avoided. Such a discussion belongs rather to the student of philosophy than of literature. My work has been to show what it was that the poet believed rather than to criticise the worth of that belief.

My method of examination is chronological. This enables me to point out the growth and developement of the poet's theory of life, and to ascertain the amount of truth in the commonplace[57] of Browning criticism, that the poet neither developed nor altered, but remained throughout on the ground taken by his first works.

In determing the periods of the poet's work I follow the excellent classification of Mr. Fotheringham which is a natural and, in fact, almost necessary one. There is no arbitrary division, on the contrary it is possible to point out the poems in which the passing of one period into the next is visible, and which thus

---

[57] First stated, I believe by Mrs. Orr in her "Handbook".

serve as links to bind the whole of Browning's work together

Period I, 1832—1840.

This period Mr. Fotheringham has well called a time of youth and prelude. It includes *Pauline, Paracelsus,* the four poems, published in *The Monthly Repository,* i. e. *The King, Porphyria, Johannes Agricola* and *"Still ailing Wind", Strafford* and *Sordello.* The characteristic of this period is its striving after the form most proper for the expression of the poet's genius. By turns the monodramatic, semidramatic[58] and narrative forms are tried. The monodramatic effectiveness of *Pauline* is weakened by a vagueness and tendency to diffusiveness, which the poet himself recognized and commented upon in the note already alluded to. *Paracelsus* ranks very high among Browning's poems, but it has little of the characteristic terseness and pungency of expression which marks his later work; and viewed as a whole there is a striking weakening of interest in the 3rd and 4th books. *Sordello,* begun, as we know from the discarded preface[59] to *Strafford* before that drama, probably in 1836, was laid aside for some time, to be completed in 1840, after his 1st Italian journey.[60] Its conception, therefore and to some extent its execution come before *Strafford* and the poems of the *Monthly Repository* which in their monodramatic and lyrical character connect this period with the second. Of the form of *Sordello* it is hardly necessary to speak at length. The heroic couplet in which it is written is no bad form for narrative, but the heroic couplet of *Sordello*

---

[58] *Paracelsus.* B. indeed declares in his preface to the 1st edition. "I have attempted to write a poem not a drama. I do not very well understand what is called a dramatic poem"; but as I have already shown B's nomenclature is not always accurate. Stedman (p. 305), in spite of B's protest, styles *Paracelsus* a drama. Bleibtreu "Geschichte der Englischen Litteratur des XIX. Jahrhunderts" S. is guilty of the same inaccuracy.

[59] Reprinted in Brown. Soc. Pap. pt. I, p. 41—42.

[60] Sharp (p. 58) asserts that *Sord.* was begun before *Paracelsus* but gives no authority for this.

would have made Pope and his followers gasp and stare,
with its breaks, dashes, run-on lines, a extra syllables.
But the special diffulty of *Sordello* is what one might
call its dramatic element and the way in which this is
introduced. In the midst of a narrative or descriptive
passage a speech is suddenly introduced, with no[60a]
indication whatever of the personality of the speaker,
and within this speech, may be found another, and
within this second a third,[60b] confusion twice confounded,
except for the most attentive reader. With this formal
is combined a textual difficulty in the extreme condensation of language, the omission of pronouns, pre-
positions relatives I conjunctions, a condensation which
has evoked the remark that the style of Sordello is
greek written in shorthand. The cause of this curious
striving after condensation on the poet's part, the more
curious as following so quickly on the easy flow of
Pauline and *Paracelsus* is said by Mrs. Orr (p. 109) to
be a criticism of John Sterling's on Browning's earlier
work. What that criticism was, she does not inform
us, but we learn from other sources that it was to the
effect that *Pauline* and *Paracelsus* revealed a tendency
to diffusiveness and redundancy of ornament which would,
if developed, lead the part astray from the paths of
pure art. It was this danger which Browning attempted
to avoid in *Sordello* and in so doing fell into the opposite
and worse extreme.

The Second Period 1841—1846 embraces the *Bells*
and *Pomegranates* series. The distinguishing notes are
dramatic and lyrical. All Browning's dramas belong
to this period with the exception of *Strafford* (which
I have already shown to be the link between this and
the foregoing) and the fragment "*In A Balcony.*" But
not only in the dramas proper is the dramatic element
found, the period of the dramatic monologue, the dramatic
lyric and romance, foreshadowed by the songs in *Para-*

[60a] See for example Gord. v. 1, p. 175.
[60b] See v. 1, p. 150 where Palma tells Gordello what Tamello
told her Ecclo's heart said to Ecclo.

celsus and by *Johannes Agricola* and *Porphyria*, begins
definitely here. The personal element which I intend
to point out in the first period, is almost entirely lacking
in this, and the argumentative, dialectical form has
not made its appearance. It is a period of purely
objective study of life with little or no effort to point
a moral or adorn a tale.

The Third Period 1846—1869 is the time of
Browning's nature and best work. It includes *Christmas
Eve and Easter Day*, the *Essay on Shelley*, *Men and
Women*, *Dramatis Personae* and *the Ring and the Book*.
A new element makes its appearance in the argumentative passages of *Christmas Eve and Easter Day*,[61] the
personal element reappears in these, in the *Essay*, in a
number of poems in *Men and Women* and *Dramatis Personae* to be pointed out hereafter, and in passages in
the Ring and the Book.

But the prevailing tone is still objective, and the
prevailing forms the dramatic monologue and lyric, the
former of which is carried to its very highest pitch of
excellence in *Karshish*, *Fra Lippo*, *Andrea*, *Cleon*, and
the great books of the *R.* and *P.*, *Caponsacchi*, *Pompilia*, the *Pope* and *Guido*. We may consider Browning
in his second and third periods, no fact, as performing
the work which he himself declared to be that of the
objective poet "one who shall replace the intellectual
rumination of food swallowed long ago by a supply of
the fresh and living swathe; getting at new substance
by breaking up the assumed wholes into parts of independent and unclassed values, careless of the unknown
laws for recombining them (it will be the business of
yet another poet to suggest those hereafter), prodigal
of objects for men's outer if not inner sight, shaping
for their uses a new and different creation from the
last, which it displaces by the right of life over

---

[61] And in such work as *Bishop Bloughram* and *Mr. Sludge*
and in the various pleas of the *Ring* and the *Book*, more especially
Tertium Puid, *Count Guido Franceschini* and the speeches of the
lawyers.

death."[62] And yet there are not wanting evidences that Browning was already arrogating to himself the work of the subjective poet of his *Essay* in whom we find "an exposition of the affinity of the creation of the objective poet to something higher, a precipitation of positive, yet conflicting facts under a harmonising law"[63] Again and again we meet with poems that are not pure objective studies of life, but an attempt to discover the "harmonising law". Little touches and reflections reveal the moral teacher behind the creator, and his interest in ethical problems steadily increases. Examples of such interested, not purely impartial work are such poems as *A Pretty Woman, The Stature and the Bust, Gold Hair* and others. Mr. Sludge is not such a purely objective study of life and the Duke in *My Last Duchess*;[64] the poem which hears his name is rather an attempt to find the law accounting for his existence.

The 4th Period, 1870—1878, Fotheringham calls "a period of later maturity". I should call it rather the period of Browning's abuse of his powers. The argumentative element wins the upper hand; the psychological analysis increases in subtlety and loses in human interest. There is a free and varied employment of form that shows the poet had new acquired a complete mastery of his modes of expression. But along with this there is a carelessness of construction and a lack of the sense of proportion which has caused some of his most unsatisfactory work. There is an almost complete disappearance of Browning's most characteristic form, the short dramatic monologue [A Forgiveness (v. 14, p. 86) is the only good example], and in a less degree of the lyric. In *R. C. N. C.* the narrative form makes its appearance for the first time since S*ord.* The personal element appears largely in *Pacch.*; and in *L. S.* we have Browning's first long autobiographical poem. The didactic tone is heard throughout, and there is a con-

---

[62] *Essay on Shelley*, Br. Soc. Pap. Pt. I, pp. 8—9.
[63] *Essay* p. 9.
[64] This poem belongs to the 2nd period (1842).

stand attempt to discover and explain the laws of existence. It is the most unsatisfactory of the periods, and ill as we could spare the poet's declaration of belief in L. S. or the lyrics scattered throughout the various volumes, it would have been better for Browning's fame had *P. H. S. Fifine* and *R. C. N. C.* never been written.

The last period, 1879—1889, regains the human interest which seemed on the point of disappearing altogether from the poet's work.

Dramatic Idylls I, which opens this period is running over with real life, and its warm reception by the critics, marks, I believe, the beginning of the poet's extended popularity in England. In the 2nd series of the Idylls a wayward humor shows itself which ran to excess in some parts of *Jocos.* and the *Parleyings.* Of this last poem and *Ferishtah* I will have to speak at such length below, that I can pass over them here with the remark that they, as the longest and most carefully planned works of this period, give it a tone of self-revelation which is utterly at variance with the poet's earlier objectivity. As works of art they do not, with the exception of a few brilliant passages in *Parleyings* and some of the lyrics in Feristah rank high among his work. In Asolando Browning's later lyric culminates in the perfect group of love songs on pp. 8—16. The light narrative form shows itself in a number of poems.[65] The dramatic element disappears almost[66] entirely (a characteristic of the whole period), and the personal tone shows itself in a number of subjective lyrics.[67]

---

[65] *The Pope and the Net* The *Beanfeast* &c. *The Cardinal and the Dog* which seems to belong to this group was written 40 years before for Willy Macready (Berdoe p. 95).

[66] *Imperante Augusto* p. 112 is the one example ot B's dramatic monologue in this volume, and the decline of his dramatic power is apparent when this poem is compared with *My Last Duchess* or *Andrea.*

[67] The Prologue, and Epilogue, and *Reverie.*

CHAPTER THIRD.

An examination of the non-dramatic poems.
Class I. The poet speaks *in propria persona.*

Ferishtah's Fancies [68]	v. 16	p. 2 ssq.
Parleyings &c.	„ 16	„ 93 ssq.

In Asolando

Prologue	p. 1
Developement	p. 131
Reverie	„ 141
Epilogue	„ 156
Why I am a Liberal-Sonnet. Berdoe [69]	„ 567
Epitaph on Levi Thaxter Mrs. Orr	„ 353

Second class. The poet uses a dramatic figure as mouthpiece.

1st Period. Pauline v. 1

a. Apostrophe to Shelley	p. 9
b. The poet's classical studies	p. 16
c. Music	„ 18
d. His devotion to Plato	„ 19
e. Caravaggio's Andromeda	p. 29—30
f. His youthful infidelity and return to faith	„ 37—38

Paracelsus v. 2

a. Rational and non-empirical nature of truth	p. 34
b. The immance of God and Nature's progression toward God	pp. 164—177

Sordello v. 1   p. 1

a. "The voice"	pp. 217—226
b. Sordello to Taurello	„ 237—238

3rd Period. By the Fireside v. 6 p. 126

Abt Vogler	„ 7	„ 101
Rabbi ben Ezra	„ 7	„ 109
R. and P. (The Pope)	„ 10	„ 64

4th Period. Balaustion   p. 11

a. Joyousness	„ 88
b. Poets	p. 110—111

---

[68] I include here the lyrics as well as the apologues.

[69] These last 2 poems come chronologically between *Ferishtah* and *Parley*. I have deferred their examination to the close of the chapter.

Particular examination of the above poems.

I. *Sordello*.[70] The poem narrates the "incidents in the developement of a soul". The main character is the Sordello mentioned by Dante (Div. commedia, Purgatorio VI, 1. 75).

The passages from this poem which I have included in the 1st class are comments by the poet himself upon his characters or on questions brought up by the story he is narrating.

a. v. 1, p. 52. Browning explains his reason for choosing the narrative instead of the dramatic form for this poem. The hero and the theme of it, being alike new to the English public, he finds it necessary to narrate, in order that he may comment and explain, rather than let the story unfold itself without his assistance.

b. v. 1, pp. 55—6. The apostrophe to Dante is quoted in all commentaries to *Sord*. With Browning's admiration for Dante expressed in it, compare

---

[70] As Sordello is the most difficult of Browning's poems I give here a number of commentaries which are of assistance. Prof. Dowden—Transcripts and Studies (London 1888). Prof. Alexander. pp. 144—177. Prof. Sonnenschein's note's (marked S) in Berdoe's article on *Sordello*. Nettleship; pp. 114—170, 201—16. Mrs. Wall Sordello's Story (Boston 1886). Jeanie Morison—Sordello—an Analysis (worthless). Mrs. Orr's "Handbook". Of these Prof. Dowden's transcript, being an analysis and running commentary of the poem, is of great value; Prof. Sonnenschein's notes are valuable for the historical allusions. Prof. Alexander's work is clear but at times too concise. Nettleship has a tendency to diffusiveness.

c. In the passage pp. 70—73 Browning describes at some length the two kind of poetical natures he has embodied in the figures of Eglamor and Sordello in the poem. Both are lovers of beauty, but the first lose themselves in their worship of it.

They are fain invest
The lifeless thing with life from their own soul

Nor rest they here, fresh birth of beauty wake
Fresh homage, every grade of love is past
With every mode of loveliness: then cast
Inferior idols off their borrowed crown
Before a coming glory. Up and down
Runs arrowy fire, whill earthly forms combine
To throb the secret forth; a touch divine —
And the sealed eyeball owns the mystic rod,
Visibly through his garden walketh God.   (p. 70—71.)

With this assertion of the immanence of God in the world which, however is only revealed to self-forgetful worshippers of beauty, compare the dying speech of Paracelsus (v. 2, p. 165 &c.).

The second class

Proclaims each new revealment born a twin
With a distinctest consciousness within
Referring still the quality, now first
Revealed, to their own soul-its instinct nursed
In silence, now remembered better, shown
More thoroughly, but not the less their own.

As love was the distinguishing quality of the first class, so is a distinct selfconsciousness the characteristic of the second. These two classes are again referred to in the opening passage of the Digression (pp. 156—157)

[70a] These verses were misinterpreted by some critics as referring to B. himself. In lines written in Miss Edith Longfellow's Autograph Album (printed in *Century* Magazine November 1882), B. corrects this mistake and names Dante.

already quoted.[71] The besetting dangers of this second class are named in this passage, and brought out at great length in the course of the poem. The first is enervation

> Ah but to find
> A certain mood enervate such a mind,
> Counsel it slumber in the solitude
> Nor stooping task for mankind's good
> Its nature. (p. 73.)

This is the temptation which is strong upon Sordello in his early days and which he overcomes when, in the camp before Ferrara, he resolves to devote himself to man (book IV). The other danger lies in the opposite extreme, in "the[72] desire to put forth all his power in this life, to display completely all the resources of a nature which can find scope for its fall developement only hereafter, and so bring ruin on himself."

> Or if yet worse befall
> And a desire possess it to put all
> That nature forth, forcing our straitened sphere
> Contain it—to display completely here
> The mastery another life should learn,
> Thrusting on time eternity's concern. (p. 73.)

d. pp. 80. Here we find the first personal utterance of Browning on Love, the conception which afterwards occupied such a position in his theory of life.

> — — — — From the beginning love is whole
> And true; if sure of nought beside, most sure,
> Of its own truth at least; nor may endure
> A crowd to see its face, that cannot know
> How hot the pulses throb, its heart below:
> While its own helplessness and utter want
> Of means to worthily be ministrant
> To what it worships do but far the more
> Its flame, exalt its idol far before
> Itself, as it would have it ever be.

It was for want of such love that Sordello's life was wasted (cf. p. 278). It is interesting to compare

---

[71] p. 37—above.
[72] Dowden—Transcripts &c.

this assertion of the entire self sacrifice of love with the passage in *R. C. N. C.* v. 12, p. 171.

    e. pp. 156—171. *The Digression.* Toward the close of the 3rd book of the poem, Browning leaves Sordello at the end of his first period of life, the self centered and introspective, and, before beginning the record of the second or altruistic period, the poet turns aside to consider his own art and its duties toward mankind. He imagines himself musing on a palace step in Venice (p. 159). First comes the passage, already[73] quoted, distinguishing between the two kinds of poets and the characteristics of their work. The truer poet, it is said, is he whose personality is not swallowed up in his work, but exists outside of it. The work of such a poet, then, may be bitful and fragmentary. Browning, who considers himself as belonging to this class, has just stopped work (as we know, in fact, that he laid *Sord.* aside to write *Strafford*, perhaps also at other times), and asks himself why he should resume it. Is there any woman adorable enough to be queen to him (p. 159), i. e. who might inspire him to continue his work for her sake. As he muses, his proper mistress, Humanity, appears to him not as he had once fancied her in ideal beauty but a sad[74] dishevelled ghost; it is for her that he will resume his task. Wretched as Humanity is,

> I love you more, for more he says to her,
> Than her I looked should foot Life's temple-floor
> Years ago. (pp. 161—2.)

i. e. real life, as he has learnt to know it is far more sympathetic to him than the dreams of his youth. He has learnt to recognise the impossibility of a life free from evil.

> Venice seems a type
> Of Life, 'twixt blue and blue extends a stripe,
> As Life, the something hangs 'twixt nought and nought.

---

[73] p. 37 above.
[74] The sad Dishevelled form wherein I put mankind. v. 1, p. 170.

'Tis Venice and 'tis life; as good you sought
To spare me the Piazza's slippery stone,
Or keep me to the unchoked canals alone,
As binder life the evil with the good
Which make up Living. (p. 161.)

Even in Evil he finds a trace of good.[75] Even in
the worst of men the sense of Right and Wrong is not
extinguished, their wrong seems to them right (p. 163)
and so long as the knowledge of the difference between
Right and Wrong remains, there is no evil which is
hopelessly incurable. Our knowledge of this fact is
but a slight advance toward remedying the evil in the
world, it is true, but slight as it is, we avoid thereby

— — — — — An ignorance increased
Tenfold by dealing out hint after hint
How nought were like dispensing without stint
The water of life—so easy to dispense
Beside, when one has probed the centre, whence
Commotion's born—could tell you of it all!
*Meantime just meditate my madrigal
O' the mugwort that conceals a dewdrop safe." (p. 164)

The meaning of this somewhat obscure passage is
as follows. There are people in the world who assert
that the problem of existence is no problem for them,
that the ills of life may be all healed by a free dis-
pensation of the "water of life",[76] and this water, they
say, is so easy to dispense when one has probed, as
they have done, to the centre of things. Yet when
they are asked for a draught of this panacea, whose
virtues they extol, they are unable to respond, except
by praises of some form which contains the merest
particle of their remedy, "the mugwort that conceals
a dew-drop safe". One cannot help thinking that there
may be an almost scornful reference in this passage to
the innumerable poem of Wordsworth, who had proclaimed

---

[75] This is the first of B's many attempts to find the low by
which evil in general, or in particular instances, may be brought
into the general scheme of good.

[76] i. e. Any imaginary remedy. The allusion is not necessarily
to dogmatic Christianity.

himself a great moral teacher, on *the Daisy, the Lesser
Celandine, the Daffodils, the Green Linnet* &c. &c. Such
assumption of omnipotence is as intolerable to us in
our struggle through life, as would have been to the
Israelites, in their sufferings in the desert of Zim, a
wiseacre who should "wonder that any one need choke
with founts about" (p. 164), and who when asked to
point out these founts should reply with "tales of
Potiphar's mishap and sonnets on the earliest ass that
spoke" (p. 164). Better than such an one would be
the Moses who should smite the rock (i. e. one who at
least strives to solve the problems that underlie man's
life); from him a thirsty people may gain "some dim
first cozings", though his awkward smiting may forfeit
for him his Promised Land (i. e. as Prof. Alexander
explains "When a poet like Browning attempts something
deeper than the superficial effusions before referred to,
when awkwardly, as all innovators, he smites the rock
and brings forth the waters of true wisdom for perishing
humanity, he finds he has sacrificed his own chances of
reward and obtained nothing in exchange, but the title
of "Metaphysic poet" p. 160). "Is not this a magnifying
of the office of the poet?" exclaims (p. 165) an objector.
"Note at all" says Browning, "in fact we can hardly
speak of such a thing as an office in this life".

> What do we here? Simply experiment
> Each on the other's power and its intent
> When else where tasked — — — — —
> — — — — — — — we watch construct,
> In short, an engine: with a finished one
> What it can do is all—nought how 'tis done.
> But this of ours, yet in probation, dusk
> A kernel of strange wheel work through its husk
> Grows into shape by quarters and by halves.
> — — — — — — — — — — — — — —
> The scope of the whole engine's to be proved;
> We die: which means to say, the whole's removed,
> Dismounted wheel by wheel, this complex gin,
> To be set up anew else where, begin
> A task indeed, but with a clearer clime
> Than the murk lodgement of our building time.
> (pp. 165—166.)

"With a fullmade machine we concern ourselves, he says, only with what it can do, but this with this growing machine it is important that we have some control over its construction, and the poet's, who see something of man's nature, can best help as by imparting to us their gift of sight."[77]

> The office of ourselves,[78] nor blind nor dumb
> And seeing something of man's state, has been
> For the worst of us to say they so have seen;
> For the better what it was they saw; the best
> Impart the gift of seeing to the rest. (p. 166.)

Note Browning's triple division of poets here, a division made rather with reference to the results obtained by the poet than one based on his method, which determines the division in the *Essay*.

In pp. 166—168 Browning proceeds to give examples of the various work of the three kinds of poets just named, and, having received the assent of an imaginary auditor to the correctness of his work, advances a step further and says

> "Thus far advanced in safety, then, proceed
> And having seen too what I saw, be bold
> And next encounter[79] what I do behold
> (That's sure) but bid you take on trust."

Note here Browning's claim for his own art. He does not submit it to the judgement of the public. "The poet", he says, "is the practised observer of life. If the public is satisfied of the truth of any of his observations, it must he content to take the rest on trust, and has no better right to cavil against them, than it has to refuse acceptance of the results of any other scientifie observer which it cannot comprehend. What is the purpose of such rights? To this question, Browning does not give a direct answer, for the answer is implied in what he has just said concerning the

---

[77] Dowden—Transcripts &c.
[78] i. e. us, the poets.
[79] Verb in imper. mood.

necessity of understanding the construction of the "machine" i. e. human character.

> Not unwisely does the crowd dispense he says
> On Salinguerras[80] praise, in preference
> To the Sordello's.

As yet the union of these two natures, the observing and the acting is unaffected,

> When at some future no-time, a brave band
> Sees, using what it sees. (p. 168.)

Then the world will no longer have need of the poet-seer. Meanwhile it behoves the world to keep these at their work. Browning himself, having been roused out of his musing by the apparition of Humanity, his mistress, will not fail in his duty;

> And therefore have I moulded, made anew
> A Man, and give him to be turned and tried,
> Be angry, or be pleased at. On your side,
> Have ye times, places, actors of your own
> Try them upon Sordello when full grown. (p. 169.)

"Here is my report", he says in other words, "on the construction of the machine. If the public refuses to recognize me as its benefactor, I will submit, nor play the part of Hercules in Egypt who came to help the natives, but when they would have sacrificed him to their prejudices, turned and slew them". With a compliment to his patron-friend[81] and to his "English Eyebright", he continues

> So to our business now—the fate of such
> As find our common nature—overmuch
> Despised, because restricted and unfit
> To bear the burden they impose on it—
> Cling when they would discard it; craving strength[86]

---

[80] Taurello Salinguerra, the Italian podesta is throughout the poem the antitype to Sordello, the man of action for action's sake as opposed to the armless dreamer.
[81] Walter Savage Landor.
[82] A pun on the name of Euphrasia Haworth.
[83] Verb in infin. mood depending on "find".

To leap from the allotted world, at length
They do leap, flounder on without a term,
Each a god's germ doomed to remain a germ,
In unexpanded infancy unless — — — — —
But that's the story. (p. 170—171.)

Here Browning sums up in a few lines the whole
purpose of this poem, which is, as Prof. Dowden has
pointed out, "to show the failure of an attempt to
manifest the infinite scope and realize the infinite energy
of will, the inability to deploy all its magnificent resources and, by compelling men to acknowledge that
nature, to gain a full sense of its existence."

f. On page 255 Browning hints at a belief of his
which he afterwards developed at greater length, i. e.
the supremacy of man over nature. The position of
those poets who assert man's littleness before "symbols
of immensity" such as sky or sea, is, he affirms false,
although specious. Browning laid such stress on the
worth of the individual that he was unable even to do
justice to the poets who forsook man to rest in nature.
This accounts partly for his intense dislike to Byron
(cf. Epilogue to *Pacch.* v. 14, p. 149; *L. S.* v. 12, p. 200;
expressed again though in dramatic form in *P. H. S.*
v. 11, p. 145—6 and *Fifine* v. 11, p. 278).

g. The passage included pp. 256—260, is of cardinal
importance to the understanding of the poem. In it
Sordello sees the truth of his whole past life revealed
to him; but as this is a particular not a general truth,
and concerned with Sordello's life not life in general,
which is the subject of our present study, we may
pass it by, only remarking on pp. 259—60 Gordello's
recognition of the fact that once he identified himself
with mankind, all is himself, all service, therefore, rates
alike. With this thought it is interesting to compare
the New Year's Hymn which is put in the month of
Pippa (v. 3, p. 13). The latter passage therefore, tho,
in form dramatic, may be considered as expressing the
poet's personal belief.

In the passage on p. 273 beginning

— — — — as who should pierce hill, plain, grove, glade,

we find one of Browning's distinct beliefs that truth
becomes more clearly seen at the approach of death.
This belief is a point which should be taken into account
when discussing the question as to whether such poems
as *A Death* &c., or such passages as the last speech
of Paracelsus are utterances of what the poet held for
truth or purely objective work.

k. Immediately on this follows a passage containing
the germ of a theory developed at great length in the
last period, namely that

> Ill and Well
> Sorrow and joy, Beauty and Ugliness
> Virtue and Vice, the Larger and the Less
> All qualities, in fine, recorded here
> Might be but modes ot Time and this one sphere
> Urgent on these, but not of force to bind
> Eternity as Time—as Matter—Mind. (p. 273.)

Grasping this truth Sordello sees the reason of
his failure. He had yielded to the second[83] danger
threatening souls like his, a danger threatening all
aspiring souls as well.

> Soul on Matter being thrust
> Joy comes when so much Soul is wreaked in Time
> On Matter: let the Soul's attempt sublime
> Matter beyond the scheme and so prevent
> By more or less that deed's accomplishement
> And Sorrow follows: — — — — — — — —
> Let the employer[84] match the thing employed[85]
> Fit to the finite his infinity
> And so proceed for ever, in degree
> Changed, but in kind the same, still limited
> To the appointed circumstance, and dead
> To all beyond. (p. 274.)

In other words it is necessary, if work is to be
done on earth, that the spiritual part of man accept
the conditions forced on him by his earthly part.
Browning is essentially an Idealist, but not a dreamer,

---

[83] See v. 1, p. 73.
[84] The soul.
[85] The body.

he recognizes the necessity of using this life, and its use is dependent upon the acceptation of its conditions.

1. On p. 278 we have one of the most important passages in Sordello.

> Ah, my Sordello, I this once befriend
> And speak for you. Of a Power above you still
> Which, utterly incomprehensible,
> Is out of rivalry, which thus you can
> Love, tho' unloving all conceived by man—
> What need! And of—none the minutest duct
> To that out—nature, nought that would instruct
> And so let rivalry begin to live—
> But of a Power its representative
> Who, being for authority the same,
> Communication different, should claim
> A course, the first chose, but the last revealed—
> This Human clear, as that Divine concealed,—
> What utter need!

The construction of this passage is extremely difficulty, but the sense is clear. The need for a man of Sordello's nature, indeed for all aspiring men, is the recognition of an absolute Power above them, incomprehensible, in the sense that they can never grasp it as they can the things of this world, and which alone, therefore, can be an object of love, as it cannot be one of rivalry. This Power is God. And besides this need there is a second, not of a communication of the nature of God, which by making him comprehensible would make him an object of rivalry, but a need of another Power, "who being for authority the same" i. e. having the same authority over man as God (for this Power is esseventially God) and yet "communicating differently", i. e. directly with us, should "claim a course", i. e. mark out a course for us to follow (cf. p. 278, 2nd line), a course which the first Power chose for us, but the last Power alone revealed, this last Human i. e. Incarnation of the Divine, being as clear, as that Divine, i. e. the absolute essence of God, is concealed. This Power is Christ.

Prof. Alexander's[86] interpretation of this passage

---

[86] Alexander, p. 176.

is the same as mine, but I have chosen to adhere more closely to the words of the text than he has done, as the difficulty here lies not so much in the abstruseness of the thought as in the uncouthness of the language in which it is couched.

The distinctly Christian sentiment of this passage is apparent. Even Mrs. Orr who endeavors wherever possible to read the Christian element out of Browning is forced here to admit this. She says:[67] "The lesson of *Sordello* is that the spiritual is bound up with the material in our earthly life. All Browning's practical philosophy is bound up in this truth, and much of his religion, for it points to the *necessity of a human manifestation of the Divine being*;[88] and though Sordello's story contains no explicit reference to Christian doctrine, an unmistakable Christian sentiment pervades its close."

m. In the closing lines of the poem, p. 289, Browning addresses half-laughingly his sleepy audience, and tells them that the story is over, and the spirit of Sordello he conjured up before them vanished, he hopes, leaving a sweet odor behind; but if the scent be rather that of a muskpod than a rose, the very pungency is a testimony to the strength of the poem and its lasting value. This same curious belief that the after effect and future potency of poetry depend upon the unpleasantness of the sensation it produces on first reading appears again in the *Epilogue* to *Pacch.* (y. 14, p. 141).

There remain in *Sordello* 2 passages of the 2nd class to consider.

a. 217—226.

Sordello had been fired with the ambition of restoring Republican Rome, but he sees that even if Rome could be restored to freedom, the degraded folk about him were no fit citizens of the Eternal City. He is on the brink of despair

---

[67] Handbook &c. p. 33.
[88] The italics are mine.

"Last of my dreams and loveliest, depart!" he says.
And then a low voice wound into his heart.

The teaching to which this voice gives utterance, whether we consider the voice to be a divine warning or the voice of his own conscience and better reason, must be that which the poet holds for truth, for the voice is not a deceiving one, but reveals to Sordello the error of his present despair, and stirs him on to the only possible right action. We are, therefore, justified in considering this voice as uttering the thoughts of the poet himself, and the passage is doubly important as being one of the few where Browning, as a rule so individualistic, reveals his interest in the collective progress of mankind.

It speaks

> Sordello, wake!
> God has conceded two rights to a man—
> One of men's whole work, time's completed plan,
> The other, of the minute's work, man's first
> Step to the plan's completeness. (p. 217.)

You have had the first right, it continues, the vision of a restored republic; this was meant to encourage you to take your first step toward its realization. The first step must be a petty one; all individual effort is petty in comparison with the amount to work to be done; but "collective man outstrips the individual" (p. 218).

In the political world to which you have now devoted yourself, there has been a toilsome but steady progress upwards. Charlemagne brought order out of chaos and founded the rule of Strength maintained by Strength (p. 219). After him Hildebrand inaugurated a new order and began the rule of knowledge maintained by Strength. Neither accomplished his work unaided. The great Kaisers developed Charlemagne's policiy, the great Pontiff's Hildebrand's. Not only these pontiffs, but workers in every degree, from Peter the Hermit to the meanest serf who recognizes in the church a power above mere force, are promoting the develope-

ment of the race. The next step will be to establish
the rule uf knowledge maintained by knowledge alone.
Toward this you, Sordello, must work. While you
remained the dreamer you might please yourself with
the creations of your fancy, but having identified yourself with the interests of mankind all is changed. Of
all mankind's wrongs you can redress but a few, but
if you will not redress these and choose to please yourself with visions of perfection, the race goes unhelped.
No dream of Rome restored will make mankind, "you
other half, stop a tear, begin a smile." And for your
first step

> Since talking is your trade
> There's Salinguerra left you to persuade (p. 225—226)

i. e. Sordello, the poet and orator, can best help the
people by persuading Salinguerra, the soldier and man
of action, to take their part.

b. The second passage p. 237—238 is by no means
so important, but contains in the mouth of Sordello a
threefold division of poets which Browning marks as
his own division by the exclamation at the close of
Sordello's characterization of the poet of the 3nd class,
"Why he writes Sordello" i. e. "This poet's task is the
very one I am new attempting". The classes are as
follows. The first simply describes men and their
characteristics, pronounces on the good or evil in their
lives, does in short the work of Dante (p. 237); the
second creates men, lets them

> — — —. love, hate, hope, fear, peace make, war wage
> In presence of you all (p. 238)

does, that is, the work of Shakespeare. The third will
"offer to unveil the last of mysteries"

> "Man's inmost life shall have yet freer play
> Once more [89] I cast external things away
> And natures composite so decompose
> That"—why he writes *Sordello*!

---

[89] i. e. Sordello, who imagines himself performing in turn
the office of each poet.

There is another passage (pp. 264—65) which, tho' belonging to neither of the classes we are examining, is yet of interest. The speech in which it occurs, Nettleship calls the speech of "the enemy". Rather it is the speech of the wavering Sordello himself. Be that as it may it represents the principle of selfishness, which tempts Sordello to abandon the cause of the people and live his own life out to the full. He rejects this temptation and tho' he dies in the struggle dies in triumph. It is plain, therefore, that the passage can only be regarded as dramatic; and yet in it are found thoughts which correspond strikingly to later views of the poet, as developed in *Ferishtah* and *Parleyings*. See the lines on Good and Evil (toward the bottom of p. 264) an the necessity of Evil to evoke Sympathy (top of p. 265) with which compare *Mihrab Shah* (v. 16, p. 37). There is evident in this latter a change of base on Browning's part.[90]

In *Sord.* alone of the poems of the 1st Period, we find the poet speaking in propria persona. But there are passages of the 2nd class which I will now compare with those already noticed.

I. *Pauline.*

a. The long apostrophe to the "Sun-treader" (pp. 9—12) shows Browning's devotion tho Shelley. We know[91] that it was to Shelley he owed his first insight into the power of poetry. With this passage we may compare the references in *Sord.*[92] v. 1, p. 53, *The Lost Leader* (v. 6, p. 7), *Memorabilia* (v. 6, p. 190) and *Cenciaja* (v. 14, p. 104), as well as the *Essay*, the greater part of which is devoted to a defense of his personal character.

b. The allusion (p. 15) to the influence of the classics on Pauline's lover may be considered as applying

---

[90] It is not the assertion of the inextricability of Good and Evil in this life that characterizes this passage in *Sord.*; nor even the thought that Evil may be but the shadow of Good, but rather the direct assertion that Good or our knowledge of it, at least, is dependent for its existence on Evil.

[91] Sharp. p. 30—32.

[92] The "spirit" is that of Shelley.

to the youthful Browning himself. During the time that
Pauline was taking shape within bis mind he attended
his only term at a University, devoting himself especially
to the study of a greek [93] under Prof. Long. But he
was already familiar with the classics through studies.
at home directed by his father, [94] and his devotion to
these showed itself in after life in the Transcriptions
from Euripides (the Alkestis in Balaustion's Adventure,
the Herakles Mainomenos in Aristophanes Apology), and
his careful and labored rendering of the Agamemnon
cf Aeschylus.

    c. Akin to this passage is the tribute to Plato
(p. 19—20). Altho' apart from this passage we have
no reference to Plato in the personal poems (the allusions
in *Ring and the Book* book 6 li 961 and *A. A.* p. v. 12,
p. 137 are dramatic), the allusion in the Essay (p. 7)
and tbe train of Idealism running through all Browning's
work (cf. especially *Abt Vogler*, v. 7, p. 101 and *R. C.
N. C.* p. 798) justify us in considering this as a direct
acknowledgement on the poet's pact of his debt to the
poet-philosopher.

    d. On pp. 17—18 we have a passage revealing
that love for music which runs so markedly through
Browning's work. We know [95] that he received careful
instruction in music, studying Harmony under Mr. John
Relfe, [96] and piano under a pupil of Moscheles. He set
a number of English lyrics to music and seems at one
time, if we may judge from the note [97] in his hand
writing on Mr. Shepherd's copy of Pauline to have
meditated musical composition on a grander scale. There
seems to be an allusion to this early hope in *One Word
More* (v. 4, p. 301)

> I shall never in the years remaining
>
> Make you music that should all-express me.

---

[93] Sharp's Life p. 34.
[94] Mrs. Orr's Life p. 33, cf. Developement *Asolando* p. 131.
[95] Mrs. Orr p. 43.
[96] Referred to v. 16, p. 224.
[97] Printed in Brown. Soc. Pap. pt. I, p. 38.

We may, therefore, I think consider the Pauline passage as personal.

> My life has not been that of those whose heaven
> Was lampless save where poesy shone out.

for all the acts shed their light upon his life, and, of all the acts, he seems to have ranked music the highest.

> Music which is earnest of a heaven
> Seeing we know emotions strange by it
> Not else to be revealed — — —[98]

e. The passage, pp. 29—30, beginning

> Andromeda and she is with me &c.

is a reference to a picture of Caravaggio, an engraving of which was in the possession of Mr. Browning,[99] or.

f. Mrs. Orr (p. 42) says that Shelley's influence on the young Browning resulted in his becoming a "professing atheist and for two years a practising vegetarian" She calls his atheism "a passing state of moral or imaginative rebellion rather than one of rational doubt", and adds that it soon cured itself. I believe traces of this period and its outcome are visible throughout *Pauline*. We see traces of his adoption of atheistic views on p. 15.

> I saw God[99] everywhere
> And I can only lay it to the fruit
> Of a sad after time *that I could doubt*
> *Even his being.*

And this doubt was, as Mrs. Orr says, rather a moral rebellion than a rational doubt, for we see on p. 15 the reference to "a neglect of all God's law" which, nevertheless, was coexistent with

> A need, a trust, a yearning after God.

---

[98] cf. *Abt Vogler* v. 7, pp. 104—105 and p. 108 also Charles Avison v. 16.

[99] Sharp. p. 25.

[99]a i. e. in early youth.

The young Browning seems in fact to have had a severe attack of Shelleyanism, a mental disease, whose symptoms may be described as a violent antipathy to all revealed religion, united to an exhibition of the highest religious feelings. From this attack, however, he soon recovered, and I believe this recovery[100] is alluded to in the passage on pp. 37—38 beginning

> Why have I girt myself in this bell-dress?

and ending

> Or witnessing thy outburst from the tomb.

Too much stress is not to be laid on the last lines of this passage (1st line of p. 38 to end of section) as an indication of the poets own belief. These represent a phase of emotional religious feeling that is by no means in accord with the poet's usual view; as may be seen by comparing them with the passage in *C. E.* (v. 5, pp. 245—251) on the Divinity of Christ, or with the strikingly un-emotional tone of *A Death* &c. (v. 7, p. 120 ssq.), dramatic though this poem be. Their tone is either due to his recent return to belief, or, as is, perhaps, more likely, his own views here are tinged by the emotional character of the person (Pauline's lover) into whose mouth they are put.

II. *Paracelsus* v. 2. This is one of the noblest of

---

[100] It is interesting to note here a passage from the *Essay* p. 15 "I shall say what I think that had Shelley lived he would finally have ranged himself with the Christians. His very instinct for helping the weaker side . . . . his very "hate of hate . . . . would have got clearer-sighted by exercise. The preliminary step to following Christ is the leaving the dead to bury their dead — not clamouring on his doctrine for a special solution of difficulties which are referable to the general problem of the Universe". He goes on to point out elements in S.'s later work that seem to him to indicate that such a change was already taking place. Now, if, as I think has been shown, B. himself once held opinions corresponding to S.'s and had come back from them to religious belief, it is easy to see the reason of his faith that S. had he lived longer would have experienced the same change. Whether this faith were well grounded or not, is not for me to determine.

Browning's poems, full of the spirit of eager effort, of zeal for humanity, and of faith in the steady progress of the world to a higher order. But its semi-dramatic form forbids as to quote at random from it as expressing Browning's views. It is the life-history of an individual soul; the character of Paracelsus is reconstructed by the poet according to his own conception of it. "The liberties which I have taken with my subject are very trifling" he says in his notes to the poem (v. 2, p. 179) "and the reader may slip the foregoing scenes between the leaves of any memoir of Paracelsus he pleases by way of commentary". It is evident, then, that the ideas of the poem are those of Paracelsus as Browning conceived him, not Browning's own, except so far as these may be identical with those of Paracelsus. If for example we quote the expression of perfect faith in God, as seen in the passage on pp. 27—28, beginning

I go to prove my soul,

as Browning's own, what is to prevent us quoting such passages as those on pp. 88 and 91 beginning

Doubts are many and faith is weak

and

You little fancy what rude shocks apprise us,[101]

as his also and charging him with inconsistency. The truth is such passages are purely dramatic, and their inconsistency is explained by the circumstances surrounding Paracelsus at the times of their utterance. What we may learn of Brownings views from this poem must be rather from a study of it as a whole than from any particular passage.

Yet there are two passages at least in the poem which may be regarded as voicing Browning's beliefs.

a. The first of these, p. 34, expresses the intuitive

---

[101] Cf. also the difference of view as to the immortality of the soul in the passages on p. 108 and p. 151.

non-empirical[102] character of truth in a way directly
parallel to that of another passage where Browning is
speaking in propria persona.

> Truth is within ourselves, it takes no rise
> From outward things — — — — — — -··
> There is an inmost centre in us all
> Where truth abides in fulness; and, around,
> Wall upon wall, the gross flesh hems it in,
> This perfect clear perception— which is truth.
>
> (v. 5, p. 250.)

With this compare the passage in *C. E.* (v. 5, p. 250)
beginning

> Take all in a word; the truth in God's breast.

So in *L. S.* the only facts the poet holds as certain
are those of which he considers himself immediately
conscious, i. e. of his own existence, and that of a
governing Power in Nature which he calls God.

b. The dying speet of Paracelsus, pp. 164—177,
is constantly quoted as expressing Browning's own views,
and I believe correctly, for when Paracelsus rouses
himself to proclaim worthily the truth toward which
he has been struggling through life, but which the
near approach of death alone has revealed, it is impossible
to resist the conclusion that the poet too accepts this
as truth. There is a fire and earnestness about the
verse that marks the language of intense conviction,
no dialectical subtleties as in *Bishop Bloughram*, but a
majesty of utterance that shows the poet has identified
himself with his hero when he says

> "here God speaks to men through me." (p. 164.)

---

[102] This passage seems to me inappropriate to Paracelsus,
the father of empiricism in modern medicine and chemistry. I
speak however with diffidence on this point. Dr. Berdoe who
has made a special study of this poem and of the character of
P. asserts p. 314 that this passage is in accordance with his
teachings. Were this not the case it would be an additional
proof that the thought here is that of B., but I believe the proof
is sufficient as it is.

It is impossible to quote the whole speech; I can only try to reproduce the chain of thought.

Paracelsus declares that "his happy time" was when he had vowed himself to man. He was born to this task, and whereas another might learn only after long struggle the purpose of life, he had always known it, with a certainty chequered by

> just so much of doubt [103]
> As bade me plant a surer foot upon
> The sun-road (p. 166)
> — — — — — I knew, I felt,
> — — — — — what God is, what we are
> What life is, how God tastes an infinite joy
> In infinite ways—one everlasting bliss
> From whom all being emanates, all power
> Proceeds; in whom is life forevermore,
> Yet whom existence in its lowest form
> Includes. (pp. 166—167.)

In the geological changes which preceed the origin of organic life in the world, and in the progress of inorganic into organic matter God rejoices. When life has appeared and the world is clothed with vegetable and over run with animal life,

> God reviews
> His ancient rapture. Thus he dwells in all,
> From life's minute beginnings, up at last
> To man—the consummation of this scheme
> Of being. (p. 168.)

Traces of man's attributes.

a) *Power*—neither put forth blindly, nor controlled
  Calmly by perfect knowledge. (p. 168)
b) *Knowledge* – not intuition, but the slow
  Uncertain fruit of an enhancing toil. (p. 169.)
c) *Love*—not serenely pure,
  But strong from weakness — — — — — —
  Love which endures and doubts and is oppressed (p. 169)

had been scattered about in Nature before; in man they

---

[103] This is one of the many indications of the speech that here we have the words of B. himself. This is his special doctrine of the function of doubt of which more hereafter.

are caught up into a unity. Nature is comprehensible only through and in Man. But progress does not stop here;

> All tended to mankind,
> And, man produced, all has its end thus far:
> But in completed man begins anew
> A tendency to God. (pp. 171—172.)

As in the lower stages there were premonitious of the coming man, so in man there arise

> August anticipations, symbols, types
> Of a dim splendour ever on before
> In that eternal circle[104] life pursues. (p. 172.)

These anticipations are found in god-like men

> Serene amid the half-formed creatures round,
> Who should be saved by them and joined with them.

To raise Man to God is to serve God truly.

> I never fashioned out a fancied good
> Distinct from Man's; a service to be done
> A glory to be ministered unto
> With powers put forth at man's expense, with drawn
> From labouring in his behalf, a strength
> Denied, that might avail him; — -- —
> — — — — — — God is glorified in man
> And to man's glory I vowed soul and limb. (p. 172—173.)

He then points out the cause of his failure. He had at first seen in Power alone

> The sign and note and character of man.

To gain Power he neglected all the teaching of the past, hoping to raise man by one grand effort to his proper place

> Of mastery o'er the elemental world. (p. 173.)

Here as in *Sord.* we are warned against the danger of refusing to submit to the conditions imposed by

---

[104] The circle from God to God, that is, for nature is here viewed as the return of the divinity to himself.

earthly life. Paracelsus had failed because of such
refusal; but he sees that the future man who shall
complete the task in which he had failed must submit
to them (p. 174). Fixing his eyes on unbounded power
alone, Paracelsus had seen his hopes perish and his
aims circumscribed, and had been on the verge of
despair, when he learnt through Aprile, the poet (whose
life and death are told in book II), "the worth of love
in man's estate"

> And what proportion love should hold with power
> In his right constitution; love preceeding
> And with more power, always much more love. (p. 175.)

But even as he had dreamed of a power above
man's, so the love he sought for in man, was super-
human, and he again refused to work under the conditions of this life;

> In my own heart love had not been made wise
> To trace love's faint beginnings in mankind
> To know even hate is but a mask of love's,
> To see a good in evil, and a hope
> In will success; to sympathize, be proud
> Of their half-reasons, faint aspirings, dim
> Struggles for truth, — — — — — — —
> All with a touch of nobleness, despite
> Their error, upward tending all though weak
>
> — — — — — — — — — — — — —
> All this I knew not and I failed. (pp. 175—176.)

The "better-tempered spirit" whom he perceives
in the future must seek at once to know and love,
and must in both submit to the conditions governing
man, while striving, none the less, to raise him to a
station where these will be no longer binding on him
(p. 176).

This passage presents many of the cardinal points
of Browning's teaching with uncommon clearness and
poetic force. The immanence of God in the world, the
conception of Evolution,[105] the value of the individual,

---

[105] The idea of Evolution is clearly stated here, tho' not in
a scientific form, 20 years before Darwin gave the results of his
investigations to the world.

the duty of the individual toward mankind, the respective worth of power[106] and love, the stress laid on the latter, and the necessity of man's submission while on earth to earth's conditions, are all insisted on here.

It is impossible, I think, that we should consider this passage where so many of the poets ideas are ideas purely dramatic.

Before leaving this period of Browning's work, let us turn back for a moment to consider it as a whole and note its general characteristics. Discarding the work which serves to link this period to the following and which, as I have shown, is in its nature dramatic and not personal, we find three long poems, *Pauline, Paracelsus* and *Sordello,* each containing the history, or a fragment thereof, of an individual soul. In *Pauline* this soul in intensely[107] self conscious, imaginative, and possessed by a yearning after God, all of which qualities do not avail to prevent its being plunged into a despair of good and a doubt of the very existence of God, from which it is only saved by the love of a woman, the Pauline, to whom the soul's confession (which constitutes the poem), is addressed. Whether the soul has been so completely restored as to perform its life work in the world is left doubtful; the conclusion of the poem wavers between a fear of relapse (p. 44) and a conviction thus.

. I shall be priest and prophet as of old (p. 45);

but at least the belief in God and in Ideal Beauty which had been shaken by contact with the realities of life is restored to the soul by earthly love.

In *Paracelsus* the soul of the hero is made of sterner stuff. He struggles against the world, hoping to win from it the secret of knowledge. It is not weakness, but an overweening and loveless ambition, an impatience of the conditions of life, which ruin him. A contrast to this nature is given us in the portrait

---

[106] Or, as it is called in the earlier books of the poems Knowledge.
[107] v. 1, pp. 14—15.

of Aprile. He "would love infinitely and he loved" (v. 2, p. 55). His devotion to Art matches that of Paracelsus to Science, but he is so intoxicated with his visions that he "cannot stoop from his sublime isolation to task himself for the good of his fellows and he sinks into a state of hopeless enervation"[108] which ends only with his death.

The character of Sordello unites the distinguishing characteristics of these three figures, the weakness of Pauline's lover, the poetical temperament of Aprile, and the boundless ambition of Paracelsus. To these he adds a selfconscious egotism which up to the last moment of his life foils every effort of his to produce a lasting effect upon the world.

It is easy to see, even from this imperfect sketch of the three poems, a common tendency running through them. In each Idealism is assumed without discussion as the proper theory of life. Not one of the four characters we have noticed is a materialist, and the chameful end of Taurello is the only warning Browning has given in this period against the danger arising from this view of life. But Idealism has also its dangers, he considers, which may, indeed, completely wreck the life of the idealist. The rude contrast between the real and the ideal may drive the soul into despair, the impossibility of attaining the ideal may lead the soul to renounce all active existence for a selfish dream-life; and lastly the over mastering power of the ideal may lead the soul to scorn all intermediate steps to its attainment, and to wreck itself in an attempt to compass the infinite at a bound. Such are the dangers that he sees in Idealism, and it is against these that the stories of Pauline's lover, Aprile, Paracelsus and Sordello warn us.

Another conception common to all three poems is the saving power of Love and its necessity to guide and sustain the idealist among the realities of life. Pauline's lover is saved from utter despair by her

---

[108] Dowden, Transcripts &c,

devotion, Paracelsus fails because of his lack of love for mankind. And the remarkable passage quoted from *Sord.* (v. 1, p. 278) shows Browning's conviction of the necessity of the love of God and the revelation of this love in human form to enable the soul to choose and hold its course through life. Sexual love, love of humanity or sympathy, and love of God or religion, are to him but varying manifestations of the same spirit. And under each aspect its saving effect upon life is ever the same. High as this estimate of love is, it is constantly increased throughout Browning, until this quality swallows up all else. "Love is enough" might be taken as the motto of his last work.

In passing to the 2nd Period of Browning's work we find a great change of tone. The form is utterly different from that of the first, and the matter is quite as much so. The poet seems to have been convinced by the ill-success of *Sord.* that be had not as yet gathered sufficient material from which to construct his theory of life. The work of this period is almost exclusively the gathering of material in the form of short objective, and as a rule dramatic, studies of life. In the few poems in which he speaks for himself there is no wrestling with the problems of life as in the 1st period, but mere touches that reveal the tend of his mind during this time of objective work.

The 1st personal poem of this period is *Waring* (v. 5, p. 78) which appeared in the 3nd number of *B. and P.*, 1842. It is a half-humourous, half-mournful lamentation over the disappearance from the London world of Browning's friend, Alfred Dommett, here called Waring.[109] He is mentioned again in *The Guardian Angel* (v. 6, p. 189). The poem is interesting as giving a picture of Browning's early life in the literary society of London about 1840, of little suppers at which the "new prose-poet" played the leading part, of the

---

[109] He seems to have been wellknown under this name to a circle of friends for B. in a letter to Miss Blagden, dated 1872, says "Waring came the other day, &c." (Mrs. Orr p. 293). See, for D.'s championship of B. against the critics, Mrs. Orr p. 111.

sundry jottings
Stray leaves, fragments, blurrs and blottings

As yet withheld from the world, but passed around among a little circle, of the eager discussion of the merit of this or that leading spirit, and of the enthusiasm for art which marked that society. Yet their seems to have been even in this society a feeling that the times were out of joint.

Who's alive?
Our men seem scarce in earnest now
Distinguished names, but tis somehow
As if they played at being names
Still more distinguished.[110]   (p. 86.)

The leading idea[111] of the poem is that a genius, such as Waring, can not be lost to the world. If he has disappeared from his old sphere it is only to re-appear elsewhere as a leading spirit

Never star
Was lost here but it rose afar!   (p. 89.)

The Boy and the Angel (v. 5, p. 19), written in 1844 for Hood's Magazine is one of the few simple narrative poems of this period. It repeats the theme of *Pippa*

All service ranks the same with God.

The boy, Theocrite, leaves his craftsman's work and cell "praise God the great way" as priest and finally as Pope. But God misses the boy's "Praise God" that used to rise at each period of his work. Gabriel takes the boy's place working and praising, but

God said "A praise is in mine ear
There is no doubt in it, no fear
— — — — — — — — — —
I miss my little human praise.

---

[110] A harsher picture of English society at this time is given by Carlyle in *Past and Present* 1843.
[111] Mr. Nettleship, pp. 59—80, has given an elaborate commentary of this poem, which is suggestive but almost too subjective to be capable of criticism.

Gabriel then goes to Rome where he finds Theocrite just made Pope. He brings him back to his craftsman's cell and early praise, taking on himself the office of Pope.[112] When Theocrite died, the angel vanished

> They sought God side by side.

5 couplets (4th, 5th and 8th on p. 22 and 1st and 3st on p. 23) added in 1845 emphasize the teaching of the poem. The 4th couplet, p. 21, was added in 1863.

The Lost Leader (v. 6, p. 7), *B.* and *P.* no. VII 1845, testifies to Browning's liberal views in politics and to his belief in the poet's duty to assist in the liberation of mankind. The change in the principles of Wordsworth[113] suggested the figure of the "lost leader". To identify Wordsworth, however, with him is going a step too far. Browning in a letter to Mr. Grosart[114] says: "I did presume to use the great and venerable personality of Wordsworth as a sort of painter's model, one from whom this or the other feature may be selected. Had I intended more—above all such a boldness as portraying the entire man, I should not have talked about "handfuls of silver &c." These never influenced the change of politics in the great poet—whose defection nevertheless, accompanied as it was, by a regular face—about of his special party was to my private apprehension and even mature[115] consideration an event to deplore. — — — Though I dare not deny the original of my little poem, I altogether refuse to have it considered the 'very effigies' of such a moral

---

[112] The 1st reading of the 2nd line of the 5th stanza on p. 23 was *Gabriel* dwelt in Peter's dome, which was altered when the poem was revised for *B.* and *P.* no. VII, 1845.

[113] His acceptance of the Laureateship in 1843 may have called forth this poem. It was regarded by the advanced liberals as putting the last seal on his defection from his early principles, already evidenced by his opposition of the Reform Bill and Catholic Emancipation.

[114] Berdoe p. 256. Cf. also B.'s letter to Miss Lee (Mrs. Orr p. 132.

[115] B. was 63 years old when he wrote these words.

and intellectual superiority". The same admiration for the qualities of the 'lost leader' is combined with the same condemnation of his defection in the poem as in this letter, in which however the bitterness of the young Browning has been softened down. Note the names of the poets whom he conceives as helping on the liberation of the world, Shakespeare, Milton, Burns, and Shelley. His optimism shows itself in the last lines of the 2nd stanza, in which he announces not only the final triumph of good, but the final[116] return of evil to good.

The 3 short poems, *Home Thoughts from Abroad* (v. 6, p. 90), *Home Thoughts from the Sea* (v. 6, p. 97), and "*Here's to Nelson's Memory*" (v. 6, p. 17), all in *B. and P.* no. VII 1845, are reminiscences of Browning's first 2 Italian journeys. The 2nd was written on shipboard[117] during his first voyage, the 1st refers to the same voyage, the 3rd to the 2nd voyage.

> T'is the *second time* that I at sea,
> Right off Cape Trafalgar here &c..

Browning's love of England shows itself in all these poems. There is a tendency to consider him at times as a poet of the world rather than of England, but only an Englishman could have written these poems. Note also in the 2nd the strong sense of duty combined with religious feeling

> "Here and here did England help me: how shall I help England"—say
> Whoso turns, as I, this evening turn to God to praise and pray.

Poems of the 2nd class I have been unable to find in this period. I have already shown how the New Year's Hymen in *Pippa* corresponds to a passage of a personal character in *Sord.* One might perhaps include this Hymn among such poems, but it is so dramatically appropriate as it stands, that I have not cared to tear it from its setting. There are passages in *Cristina* (v. 6, p. 39) that coincide closely with views expressed

---

[116] Cf. last stanza of *Apparent Failure* (v. 7, p. 246).
[117] Mrs. Orr p. 101.

elsewhere by the poet; but the dramatic character of this poem is sufficiently indicated by its 1st title in *B. P.* (no. VII) i. e. *Queen Worship.* The views expressed in this poem then as to love and immortality may only be accepted as the poet's own, in so far as they agree with direct statements of his elsewhere. Such in fact is the character of this whole period; my scanty use of its materials might lead to the mistaken belief that little was to be learned from it. Much is to be learnt concerning Browning's beliefs from *Pippa Cristina*[118] *Colombe's Birth day, Pictor Ignoties* (v. 4, p. 202), *The Flight of the Duchess* (v. 5, p. 116), *Luria* and *a Soul's Tragedy* (v. 3, p. 257).

But I have preferred to pass over all poems of a distinctly dramatic nature, and construct Browning's theory of life from utterances undeniably his own.

----

[118] See Nettleship's examination of this poem and *The Flight* &c. pp. 13—16, and pp. 46—59.

A Bibliography

of

Robert Browning.

I. Browning's Works.

1833. 1. Pauline—a Fragment of a Confession.[1]
1834. 2. Sonnet. "Eyes calm beside thee"
      In *Monthly Repository* for August 1834; signed Z.[2]
1835. 3. Paracelsus.[3]
    4. The King.
      In *Monthly* Repository for signed Z.[4]
1836. 5. Porphyria.
      Monthly Repository for signed Z.[5]
    6. Johannes Agricola
      Monthly Repository for signed Z.[6]

---

[1] Only 5 copies extant, 3 in the British Museum. Reprinted for 1st time in 1868; revised in 1888—89.

[2] Reprinted—Berdoe p. 477.

[3] Preface to 1st edition reprinted in Brown. Soc. Pap. pt. I. pp. 38—39.

[4] Afterwards incorporated with additions (6 lines) and changes in *Pippa* act III, sc. I.

[5] Reprinted in *B. and P.* no. III, as no. 2 ot Madhouse cells; in 1863 and after called *Porphyria's Lover*.

[6] Reprinted in *B. and P.* no. III, as no. of Madhouse cells; in 1863 and after called J. A. in Meditation.

7. "Still ailing, Wind?"
   Monthly Repository signed Z.[7]
8. A Life of Strafford
   In Lordner's Cabinet Cyclopaedia. Lives of
   Eminent British Statesmen. v. 2, pp. 178—411.
   By John Forster.[8]

1837. 9. Strafford—an historical Tragedy
   The preface omitted in 1863; is reprinted in
   Brown. Soc. Pap. pt. I, pp. 41—42.

1840. 10. Sordello.

1841—1846. Bells and Pomegranates.

1841. 11. *B.* and *P.* no. I. Pippa Passes.[9]

1842. 12. „ „ „ „ II. King Victor and King Charles.
   „ „ „ „ III. Dramatic Lyrics containig.
   13. Cavalier Tunes
      I. Marching along
      II. Give a Rouse
      III. My Wife Gertrude.[10]

ITALY AND FRANCE.

14. I. Italy.[11]
15. II. France.[12]

---

[7] Reprinted as 1st 6 stanzas of § 6 of James Lee in *Dram. Pers.*

[8] This "Live" is now known to have been written by Browning for his friend Forster, who had undertaken the work, but owing to illness was not able to complete it in the specified time. Dr. Furnivall first stated this fact, on B.'s authority in a letter to the Pall-Mall Gazette, Apr. 1890. Dr. F. asserts that B.'s work begins p. 182 with the words "James 1 came to this &c." For fuller discussion of question see Berdoe p. 526—530. The "Life" has recently been published by Smith, Elder and Co. uniform with the last edition of B.'s works.

[9] Advertisement and dedication to Serjeant Talfourd reprinted in Brown. Soc. Pap. pt. I, p. 44.

[10] III is called in 1849 and after *"Boot and Saddle"*.

[11] in 1849 called "My Last Duchess"; in 1863 and after "M. L. D.—*Ferrara*".

[12] in 1849 called Count Gismond; 1863 and after "C. G. — *Aix in Provence*".

CAMP AND CLOISTER.

16. I. Camp (French).[13]
17. II. Cloister (Spanish).[14]
18. In a Gondola.
19. Artemis Prologuizes.
20. Waring.

QUEEN-WORSHIP.

21. I. Rudel and the Lady of Tripoli.[15]
22. II. Cristina.

MADHOUSE-CELLS.

5. I. "There's heaven above".
6. II. "The rain set early in to-night".
1842. 23. *Through the Metidja to Adb-el-Kadr, 1842.*
24. The Pied Piper of Hamelin;[16]
a Child's Story.
1843. 25. *B. and P.* no. IV—The Return of the Druses
—a Tragedy in 5 Acts.
26. *B. and P.* no. V. A Blot in the Scutcheon;
a Tragedy in 3 Acts.
1844. 27. *B. and P.* no. VI. Columbe's Birth day—
a play in 5 Acts.

IN HOOD'S MAGAZINE.

June 1844.
28. The Laboratory (Ancien Régime).
July.
29. Claret and Tokay.[17]

---

[13] In 1849 and after called *"An Incident of the French Camp"*
[14] In 1849 and after called "A Soliloquy of the Spanish Cloister"
[15] Called in 1849 and after "*R. to the L. of T.*"
[16] Der Rattenfänger von Hameln.
[17] Called in 1863 and after *"Nationality in Drinks"*

30. Garden Fancies.
    I. The Flower's Name.
    II. Sibrandus Schnafburgensis.
    August.
31. The Boy and the Angel.
1845. March.
    32. The Tomb at St. Praxed's.[18]
    April.
    32a. The Flight of the Duchess, pt. I, 9 §.[19]
        B. and P. no. VII. Dramatic Romances and
        Lyrics.
    34. "How they brought the good news from Ghent
        to Aix".
    35. Pictor Ignotus (Florence 15—).
    36. Italy in England.[20]
    37. England in Italy—Piano di Sorrento.[21]
    38. The Lost Leader.
    39. The Lost Mistress.

HOME THOUGHTS FROM ABROAD.

40. I. "Oh, to be in England".
41. II. "Here's to Nelson's memory".[22]
42. III. "Nobly Cape St. Vincent."[23]
32. The Tomb at St. Praxed's.
30. Garden Fancies I and II.

FRANCE AND SPAIN.

28. I. The Laboratory (Ancien Régime).
42. II. The Confessional.
33 a and b. The Flight of the Duchess.
    § 10—16 new.

---

[18] Called in 1849 and after *"The Bishop order his T. at St. P.'s Church"*.
[19] Reprinted with pt. II, § 10—16, in *B and P.* no. VII.
[20] Called in 1849 and after *"The Italian in England"*.
[21] Called after 1849 *"The Englishman in Italy"*.
[22] Included under *"Nationality in Drinks"* in 1863, being no. III *"Beer"*.
[23] after 1849 called *"Home Thoughts from the Sea"*.

44. Earth's Immortalities
    I. Fame.
    II. Love.
45. Song "May but you &c."
31. The Boy and the Angel
    with 5 new couplets.

NIGHT AND MORNING.

46. I. Night.[24]
47. II. Morning.
29. Claret and Tokay.
48a. Saul pt. I. § 1—9.
49. Time's Revenges.
50. The Glove (Peter Ronsard loquitur).
1845. B and P. no. VII.
51. Luria—a Tragedy in 5 acts.
52. A Soul's Tragedy.[25]
1849. Poems—2 vols, containing.
    I. Paracelsus.
    II. B. and P. except 29 and 41.
1850. 53. Christmas Eve and Easter Day—a Poem.
1852. 54. An Introductory Essay to 25 (spurious) letters of Shelley; reprinted by Brown. Soc. Pap. pt. I.[26]
1854. 55. The Twins, published in a booklet in behalf of the Ragged Schools.[27]
1855. 56. Men and Women, containing Love among the Ruins.
57. A Lovers' Quarrel.
58. Evelyn Hope.
59. Up at a Villa—Down in the city (as distinguished by an Italian person of quality).
60. A Woman's Last Word.

---

[24] After 1849 these are called "*Meeting and Night*" and "*Parting at Morning*".
[25] Preface to 52 explaining title of *B. and P.* reprinted in Brown. Soc. Pap. pt. I, p. 51.
[26] Also by Smith, Elder and Co. 1888.
[27] See Berdoe p. 551.

1855. 61. Fra Lippo Lippi.
    62. A Toccata of Galuppi's.
    63. By the Fireside.
    64. Any Wife to any Husband.
    65. An Epistle concerning the strange Medical Experience of Karshish, the Arab Physician. [28]
    66. Mesmerism.
    67. A Serenade at the Silla.
    68. My Star.
    69. Instans Tyrannus.
    70. A Pretty Woman.
    71. "Childe Roland to the Dark Tower came" (See Edgar's song in *Lear*).
    72. Respectability.
    73. A Light Woman.
    74. The Statue and the Bust.
    75. Love in a Life.
    76. Life in a Love.
    77. How it strikes a Contemporary.
    78. The Last Ride Together.
    79. The Patriot (An old Story).
    80. Master Hugues of Saxe-Gotha.
    81. Bishop Bloughram's Apology.
    82. Memorabilia.
    83. Andrea del Sarto (called the Faultless Painter).
    84. Before.
    85. After.
    86. In Three Days.
    87. In a Year.
    88. Old Pictures in Florence.
    89. In a Balcony.
    48a and b. Saul. § 1—9 revised, § 10—19 new.
    90. De Gustibus.
    91. Women and Roses.
    92. Protus.
    93. Holy Cross Day (On which the Jews were forced to attend an annual Christian sermon in Rome).

---

[28] Generally quoted as "*Karshish*".

1855. 94. The Guardian Angel—a Picture at Fano.
     95. Cleon.[29]
     55. The Twins.
     96. Popularity.
     97. The Heretic's Tragedy—a Middle Age Interlude.
     98. Two in the Campagna.
     99. A Grammarian's Funeral (Time—shortly after the Introduction of Learning in Europe).
    100. One Way of Love.
    101. Another Way of Love.
    102. Transcendentalism—a Poem in 12 books.
    103. Misconceptions.
    104. One Word More—To E. B. B.[30]
1856. 105. Ben Karshook's Wisdom—Printed in the "Keepsake" for 1856.[31]
1857. 106. May and Death. In the "Keepsake" for 1857.[32]
1863.   Poetical Works cf. R. B. 3 vols, containing all previous poems but 1, 2, 105 and 106.
1864.   Dramatis Personal, containing
    107. James Lee,[33] 9 §. 6 reappears as the first 6 stanzas of § 6.
    108. Gold Hair—A Legend of Pornic.[34]
    109. The Worst of It.
    110. Dis aliter Visum or Le Byron de nos Jours.
    111. Too Late.
    112. Abt Vogler—(after he has been extemporizing on the musical instrument of his invention).
    113. Rabbi ben Ezra.

---

[29] Printed before appearance of *M. and W.* as a brochure by Moxon and in the "Atlantic Monthly".

[30] Elizabeth Barrett Browning.

[31] Reprinted in Mrs. Orr p. 205.

[32] Reprinted in *Dram. Person.* 1864.

[33] Reprinted in 1863 as James Lee's Wife. § 6 first printed in Atlantic Monthly v. 13, 1864. Part 2 of § 8 expanded in 1868 from 2 to 63 lines.

[34] First printed in Atlantic Monthly v. 13, 1864. 3 new stanza added in 1868.

1864. 114. A Death in the Desert.
     115. Caliban upon Setebos—or Natural Theology in the Island.
     116. Confessions.
     106. May and Death.
     117. Prospice.[35]
     118. Youth and Art.
     119. A Face.
     120. A Likeness.
     121. Mr. Sludge, the Medium.
     122. Apparent Failure.
     123. Epilogue.
     124. Orpheus and Eurydice—For a picture by Leighton, printed in the Royal Academy Catalogue for 1864 as prose; in 1868 included in *Dram. Pers.* and called "E. to. O."

1868.   Poetical Works. 6 vols, containing all former poems but 2 and 105, and 1 new poem, namely
     125. Deaf and Dumb—for a group by Woolnes.

1868—69. 126. The Ring and the Book.

1871. 127. Hervé Riel. In Cornhill Magazine March 1871, reprinted in *Pacchiarotto* &c.
     128. Balaustion's Adventure, including a Transcript from Euripides.[36]
     129. Prince Hohenstiel-Schwangau, Saviour of Society.

1872. 130. Fifine at the Fair.
     Prologue—Amphibian.
     Epilogue Householder.

1873. 131. Red Cotton Night Cap Country—or Turf and Towers.

1875. 132. Aristophanes' Apology—including a Transcript[37] from Euripides; being the last Balaustion.

---

[35] Frist printed in the Atlantic Monthly v. 13, 1864.
[36] A Translation of E.'s "Alkestis".
[37] A Translation of E.'s "Herakles Mainomenos".

1875. 133. The New Album.[38]
1876.　　　Pacchiarotto and how he worked in Distemper; with other Poems, containing
　　　134. Prologue.
　　　135. Pacchiarotto and how he worked &c.
　　　136. At the Mermaid.
　　　137. House.
　　　138. Shop.
　　　139. Pisgah Sights.
　　　　　I. "Over the ball of it".
　　　　　II. "Could I but live again".
　　　140. Fears and Scruples.
　　　141. Natural Magic.
　　　142. Magical Nature.
　　　143. Bifurcation.
　　　144. Mempholeptos.
　　　145. Appearances.
　　　146. St. Martin's Summer.
　　　127. Hervé Riel.
　　　147. A Forgiveness.
　　　148. Cenciaja.
　　　149. Filippo Baldinucci on the Privilege of Burial (A Reminiscence of A. D. 1676).
　　　150. Epilogue.
1877. 151. The Agamemnon of Aeschylus—transcribed by R. B.
1878.　　　La Sasiaz: The Two Poets of Croisic.
　　　152. La Sasiaz (To A. E. S.),[39] Poem "Good to forgive".
　　　153. The Two Poets of Croisic. Proem. "Such a starved bank &c." Epilogue "What a pretty tale".
1879. 154. "The Blind Man to the Maiden said" (Translation of a poem of Wilhelmine v. Hillern). In Clara Bell's[40] translation of the Hour will come.

---

[38] There is a good german translation of this by E. Leo, Hamburg, 1877.
[39] Anne Egerton Smith.
[40] Reprinted in Brown. Soc. Pap. pt. 4, p. 410.

1879. 155. Oh, Love, Love!
A translation of ll. 525 ssq. of the Hippolytus
of Euripides. In J. P. Mahaffy "Euripides"
(London 1879).[41]

DRAMATIC IDYLLS, CONTAINING.

156. Martin Relph.
157. Pheidippides.
158. Halbert and Hob.
159. Ivàn Ivànovitch.
160. Tray.
161. Ned Bratts.

DRAMATIC IDYLLS SECOND SERIES, CONTAINING

1880. 162. Proem—"You are sick &c."
163. Echellos.
164. Clive.
165. Mulêykeh.
166. Pietro of Abano.
167. Dr—
168a. Epilogue "Touch him ne'er so lightly".
1882. 168b. "So I wrote in Venice"; being 10 new lines
to 168a, written for Miss Longfellow, published
in "Century Magazine" vol. 25, p. 159.

JOCOSERIA—CONTAINING.

1883. 169. Wanting is—What?
170. Donald.
171. Salomon and Balkis.
172. Cristina and Monaldeschi.
173. Mary Wollestonecraft and Fuselli.
174. Adam, Lilith and Eve.
175. Ixion.
176. Jochanan Hakkadosh.[42]

---

[41] Reprinted in Brown. Soc. Pap. pt. 1, p. 69.
[42] In the notes to this poem v. 15, appear 3 burlesque
sonnets 1. "Moses the weck." 2. "And this same fact, &c."
3. "Og's Highbone."

1883. 177. Never the Time and the Place.
     178. Pambo.

     180. Sonnet on Goldoni. Written for the Album of the Committee for the G. monument at Venice. [43]

     181. Sonnet on Rawdon Brown; dated Nov. 8th 1883. Printed first in Century Magazine v. 27, p. 640.

     182. Paraphrase from Horace.
        An impromtu translation for Felix Moscheles. Printed first in Pall-Mall Gazette Dec. 13 1883.

     183. Helen's Tower—A Sonnet (Dated 1870). First printed in Pall-Mall Gazette Dec 28th 1883. [43a]

1884. 184. The Founder of the Feast—A Sonnet Dated Apr. 5th 1884. First printed in "The World" Apr. 16th 1884.

     185. The Names—A Sonnet. First printed in Pall-Mall Gazette May 29th 1884.

     186. An Introduction to "The Divine Order and other Sermons by Thomes Jones" (London 1884).

     187. Feristah's Fancies, [44] containing Prologue.
        The Eagle
          Lyric: "Round us the wild creatures".
        The Melon-Seller
          Lyric: "Wish no word unspoken".
        Shab Abbas
          Lyric: "You groped your way".
        The Family
          Lyric: "Man I am".
        The Sun
          Lyric: "Fire is in the flint".

---

[43] Reprinted Mrs. Orr, p. 358.
[43a] Reprinted Mrs. Orr, p. 285,
[44] I have not numbered the apologues and lyrics of this volume eparately, for they are not distinct poems but parts of a whole.

1884.   Mihrab Shah
       Lyric: "So the head aches".
    A Camel-Driver
       Lyric: "When I vexed you".
    Two Camels
       Lyric: "Once I saw a chemist".
    Cheries
       Lyric: "Verse-making".
    Plot.-Culture
       Lyric: "Not with my Soul".
    A Pillar at Sebzevar
       Lyric: "Ask not one least &c."
    A Bean-Stripe—also Apple-Eating
       Lyric: "Why from the world".
    Epilogue.

1885. 188. Epitaph on Levi Thaxter.
       Dated April 19th 1885. First printed in
       Mrs. Orr p. 353.

    189. Why I am a Liberal—Sonnet.
       Printed[45] in a pamphlet of the same title,
       edited by A. Reid (London 1886).

1886. 190. Lines—"Danse yellows and whites and reds".
       First printed in the "New Amphion", a booklet
       gotten up for the benefit of the Edinburgh
       University Union's Fancy-Fair 1886. Re-
       printed at the close of Gerard de Lairesse
       in Parleyings v. 16, p. 219.

1887. 191. Parleyings with certain People of Importance
       in their Day; containing
       Apollo and the Fates—a Prologue.
       With Bernard de Mandeville.
       With Daniel Bartoli.
       With Christopher Smart.
       With George Bubb Doddington.
       With Francis Furini.
       With Gerard de Lairesse.

---

[45] Reprinted in Berdoe p. 567 and in the last volume of the American Edition (Houghton Mifflin and Co.) of B.

With Charles Avison.
First and his Friends—an Epilogue.

1889. 192. Prefatory note to "The Poetical. Works of Elizabeth Barrett B." (London 1889).

193. Lines to Edward Fitzgerald.[46]
In the "Athenaeum" of July 13th 1889.

1888—89. Robert Browning's Poetical Works. 16 vols. (The standard edition.)

1889. Asolando-Facts and Fancies containing[47]

194. Prologue "The Poet's age".
195. Rosny.
196. Dubiety.
197. Now.
198. Humility.
199. Poetics.
200. Summum Bonum.
201. A Pearl—a Girl.
202. Speculative.
203. White Witchcraft.
204. Bad Dreams.
   I. "Last night I saw you".
   II. "You in the flesh and here."
   III. "This was my dream".
   IV. "It happened thus".
205. Inapprehensiveness.
206. Which.
207. The Cardinal and the Dog.[48]
208. The Pope and the Net.
209. The Bean-Feast.
210. Muckle-Mouth Meg
211. Arcades Ambo.
212. The Lady and the Painter.

---

[46] No friend of B. can wish to see these unfortunate lines preserved, but 1 have not the right to exclude them from what wishes to be a complete bibliography. As to their occasion see Mrs. Orr p. 422.

[47] This volume appeared in London Dec. 12th 1889, the day of B.'s death.

[48] Written ca. 1840 for William Macready jr. (see Mrs. Orr pp. 131—132.

213. Ponte dell' Angelo—Venice.
214. Beatrice Signorini.
215. Flute-Music, with an Accompaniment.
216. "Imperante Augusto Natus Est".
217. Developement.
218. Rephan.
219. Reverie.
220. Epilogue.

———

II. Biography, Criticism &c.

The following bibliography can not lay pretense
to completeness as new works on Browning are constantly issuing from the press. All books, but one,
included in it were in the British Museum in the Autumn
of 1892 and have been personally examined.

a) Biographical.

1. *Mrs. Orr.* "Life and Letters of R. B." London
   1891. This is the standard and authorized
   biography. Mrs. Orr's intimate acquaintance
   with the poet enables her to speak with authority
   as to his private life. Nevertheless the work is
   disappointing, ane one cannot help wishing that,
   especially in the last years of his life, she had
   allowed the poet to speak more frequently for
   himself in the form of letters or records of con-
   versations, for which we could have spared many
   of her subjective judgements as to the poet and
   the qualities of his work.

2. *William Sharp.* "Life of R. B." London 1890.
   A capital little book especially in its criticisms
   of B.'s earlier work. The latter is somewhat
   slurred of, doubtless from the write's desire to
   consider B. as a poet rather than a philosopher.
   An elaborate Bibliography by Mr. Anderson of
   the British Museum adds value to the book.

3. *Thomas Powell.* "The Living Authors of England." New York 1849. A wretched bit of back work.
4. "A Few Words on *R. B.*" Philadelphia 1890. I suspect the writer to be Dr. Furness; it is a clever, witly and scholarly little book, with an interesting record of the writer's acquaintance with B.
5. *Edwin Gosse.* "R. B.—Personalia". London 1890. This is practically a reprint of an article in the *Century Magazine* Dec. 1881; the added chapter on "Personal Impressions" is of little value compared with the first which contains facts as to B.'s early life obtained by G. from B. himself.
6. *Joseph Jacobs.* "Essays and Reviews". London 1890. Containing B.'s obituary in the Athenaeum.

b) Books of Reference.

1. *Mrs. Orr "Handbook* to R. B.'s Works". London 1886. This book contains an introduction to Browning and a more or less complete analysis of his works up to 1886. Its great fault is its failure to explain the references and allusions which are as a rule the most puzzling things in B.'s work.
2. *Dr. Berdoe.* "The B. Cyclopedia". London 1892; 2nd edition. This is a work at once most valuable and most untrustworthy. It gives a mass of information as to Browning, prints a number of his letters; gives an analysis (as a rule inferior to Mrs. Orr's) of each poem, and explains many of the references. It is, however, full of the most glaring errors, especially in all that relates to classical literature and history, some of which have been corrected by Prof. Jones in the Corrigenda et Addenda prefixed (p. XXI) to the 2nd edition. An over-large number however still remain.
3. *George W. Cook.* "A Guide book to the poetic and dramatic Works of R. B." Boston 1891.

This is an American counterpart to Berdoe's
Cyclopedia. Its references are to the American
edition (Houghton Mifflin and Co.) of B. Dr.
Furnivall ranks it below Berdoe. I have found
no such glaring errors in it although it contains
a mass of absolutely unnecessary information.

c) Introductions to Browning.

1. *Prof. Corson.* "An Introduction to the Study of
   R. B.'s Poetry". Boston 1886. A suggestive,
   yet unsatisfactory book, uniting original thought
   with a tendency toward the diffusive common
   place. It contains also 32 poems of B.'s with
   notes.
2. *Bancroft Cooke.* "An Introduction to R. B."
   London (?) 1883. Valueless.
3. *Arthur Symons.* "An Introduction to the Study
   of B." London 1886. A capital little book,
   written from the aesthetical critic's point of
   view, and ignoring, perhaps too much, B's importance as a thinker.
4. *Prof Alexander.* "An Introduction to the Poetry
   of R. B." Boston 1889. This work was originally
   delivered in the form of lectures to the writers
   students. It is beyond doubt the best text-book
   on Browning. Its weakness lies in its hasty
   treatment of the latter periods of B.'s work.
5. *F. Mary Wilson.* "A Primer on B." London
   1891. An ill-arranged and scrappy book, but
   with valuable notes; all references are to the
   last edition of B.

d) Studies of separate poems, introductions to selections &c.

1. Strafford. Edited by Miss Hickey (London 1884)
   with a valuable introduction by Prof. Gardiner.
2. Sordello, being pp. 474—525 of "Transcripts
   and Studies" by Prof. Dowden (London 1888).
3. Sordello—an Analysis—Jeanie Morison (Edinburgh 1890). Worthless.
4. Sordello's Story—Annie Wall (Boston 1886).
5. "Sordello" being pp. 221—260 of "Dante and

other essays" by R. W. Church (London 1888).
Very good.

6. Introductory Essay to "Christmas Eve and Easter-
Day and other Poems" by Heloise Heisey
(Boston [?]). Very good.

7. Of Fifine, Christmas Eve and Easter-Day and
other Poems—Jeanie Morison (Edinburgh 1892).
Worthless.

8. A Blot in the Scutcheon[49]—edited by Wm. Rolfe
and Heloise Hersey. Valuable introduction, containing letter from Lawrence Barrett on the
scenic possibilities of "The Blot"; good notes,
capital school-edition.

9. A Selection from B. F. H. Ahn (Berlin, Fried-
berg und Mode). With a memoir and explana-
tory notes, not always accurate.

10. Selections from the Poetry of R. B.—With a
very good Introduction by R. G. White (New
York 1883).

11. Our Living Poets H. Buxton Forman (London
1871). Largely an appreciative review of *The
Ring and the Book*.

e) General criticism.

1. B. as a Philosophical and Religious Teacher—
Prof. Jones (Glasgow 1891). By far the best
book on the subject; a careful examination of
B.'s teachings from the standpoint of a student
of philosophy.

2. Four Great Teachers—Joseph Forster (London
1890). Worthless.

3. Sermons from B.—F. Ealand (London 1892). Of
no great value.

4. The Religion of our Literature.[50] Rev. George
Mac Crie (London 1875). A very keen attack
on B. from the standpoint of the narrowest
Calvinism.

---

[49] Including "Colombe" and "A Soul's Tragedy".
[50] The essay on Tennyson contained in this book is one of
the most amusing pieces of writing extant.

5. Mr. Tennyson and Mr. B.—Prof. Dowden. Dublin After noon Lectures (Dublin 1869). A very good study.
6. On some Points in B.'s View of Life—B. F. Westcott (Cambridge 1883). Commonplace.
7. B.'s Message to his Times. Dr. Berdoe (London 1890). Interesting as treating B. from the standpoint of a practical scientist, as literary criticism weak.
8. B.'s Criticism of Life. Wm Revell (London 1892).
9. B.'s Women. M. E. Burt (Chicago 1887). Probably the worst book on B. yet written; absolutely valueless.
10. Studies in the Poetry of R. B.—J. Fotheringham (2nd edition London 1888): A capital series of studies, marked by much taste and judgement, handling B. from the aesthetical rather than the ethical side.
11. R. B.—Essays and Thoughts. J. T. Nettleship (revised edition, London 1890). It is extremely difficult to criticise this book. Its paraphrases of various poems are at times valuable; but its tone is so subjective, that it often withdraws itself from the field of literary criticism. It is suggestive, rather than instructive.
12. R. B.—Chief Poet of the Age. W. G. Kingsland (London 1887). Of small worth.
13. Stories from R. B. Frederick May Holland (London 1882). Introduction by Mrs. Orr. A pleasing little book modelled on Lamb's Tales from Shakespeare.
14. Essays on English Literature—Thomas Mc.—Nicoll (London 1861).
15. Papers on Literature and Art—Margaret Fuller (London 1846). "B.'s poems" pp. 31—45. Valuable as testifying to B.'s early popularity in America.
16. A New Spirit of the Age—edited by R. H. Home (London 1844). "R. B. and J. W. Marston" pp. 155—186. A review of B.'s early works, marked by an instinctive sense of B.'s power.

. 7

17. Literary Essays—R. H. Hutton (London 1888).
18. Literary Studies—Walter Bagehot (London 1879). See my note on pp. 2—3 above.
19. Urbana Scripta—Studies of Five Living Poets. A Galton (London 1885).
20. Studies in Letters and Life. G. Woodberry (Boston 1890). The essay on B.'s death, pp. 276—296 shows considerable insight though it makes the old mistake of charging B. with false moral teaching basing this charge on the Statue and the Bust.
21. A comparative Estimate of Modern English Poets —J. Devey (London 1873). A thoroughly Philistine bit of criticism.
22. Poets in the Pulpit.—H. R. Haweis (London 1880). B. pp. 119—143.
23. Philosophy and Religion Rev. A. H. Strong (New York 1888). pp. 525—543. "The poetry of R. B." Interesting as showing P.'s power of attracting even the narrowest theological mind.
24. Essays on Poets and Poetry—Roden Noel (London 1886).
25. Chapters on English Metre—Joseph Mayor (London 1886). pp. 192—196 an examination of B.'s blank verse.
26. Victorian Poets—E. C. Stedman (revised edition, Boston 1887). See pp. 1—2 above.
27. Poets and Problems—G. W. Cooke (Boston 1886). B. pp. 271—388. A thought ful and suggestive essay.
28. George Chapman—Works; in 3 vols. In the introduction by A. C. Swinburne occurs (p. XIV ssq.) a discussion of B.'s obscurity which displays Swinburne's fine critical insight.
29. La Renaissance de la Poésie Anglaise—Gabriel Sarrazin (Paris 1889). A brilliant study of B. as the creator of the psychological drama.

The papers of the Browniug Society are of the greatest value to the student, but are naturally of varying worth, ranging from fine critical studies of individual poems to the weakest of gush on B. in general.

The articles on B. contained in Magazines are innumerable and as a rule do not repay the reading. Dr. Furnivall has a "Trial-List" of them (Brown. Soc. Pap. pt. I) up to 1882, Mr. Anderson in Sharpe's "Life of B." up to 1890.

VITA.

I was born at Dayton, Ohio (U. S. A.) on the 22nd of December, 1866 and am a member of the Presbyterian Church of America. I pursued my primary studies at home, prepared for college at the Deaver Collegiate Institute of Dayton, Ohio, and at the Morristown Academy, Morristown, New Jersey. I matriculated at the College of New Jersey, Princeton, New Jersey, in September 1884, where I pursued the Academic 4 years course, graduating *cum laude* in June 1888, with the degree of A. B. I tought for two years in the Preparatory Department of Miami University, Oxford, Ohio; and then came to Europe. In October 1890 I entered the University of Leipzig, where I have since remained. I have attended courses under Profs. Wülker, Zarncke, Maurenbrecher, Birch-Hirschfeld, Sievers and Heinze, and Privat-Docenten Flügel, Witkowski, Weigand and Brockhaus. I have been a member of the English Seminar under Prof. Wülker since its organization, and have also been a member of the Romance Seminar under Prof. Birch-Hirschfeld, and of the German Proseminar under Prof. Sievers.

www.ingramcontent.com/pod-product-compliance
Lightning Source LLC
Chambersburg PA
CBHW032157010726
47493CB00008BA/2732